THE GUNSMITH

456

The Daughter of Jean Lafitte

Books by J.R. Roberts
(Robert J. Randisi)

The Gunsmith series

Lady Gunsmith series

Angel Eyes series

Tracker series

Mountain Jack Pike series

COMING SOON!

The Gunsmith
457 – The Guns of St. Augustine

For more information visit:
www.SpeakingVolumes.us

THE GUNSMITH

456

The Daughter of Jean Lafitte

J.R. Roberts

SPEAKING VOLUMES, LLC
NAPLES, FLORIDA
2020

The Daughter of Jean Lafitte

ISBN 978-1-64540-194-0

Chapter One

At sixty-one years old, Marguerite Lafitte was still a stunning beauty. Many of the businessmen in New Orleans were still bombarding her with proposals of marriage, but she was fending them off not only for herself, but for her daughter, as well. Angelique was a breathtaking beauty in her twenties, and together the two women robbed the men of New Orleans of not only their breath, but their senses, as well . . .

***

The two Lady Lafittes entered their home in the Garden District, removed their wraps and gloves.

"How many?" Marguerite asked her daughter. "How many asked tonight?"

"Oh, Mama," Angelique said, "what does it matter? None of them are worthy, are they?"

"Not of us," Marguerite said. "Not of you, my love."

"I'm tired," Angelique said. "I'm going to bed Mama. I will see you in the morning."

She kissed her mother's cheek and went upstairs to her room.

Marguerite went into the drawing room and poured herself a glass of brandy from the crystal decanter on the sideboard. Then she sat in her favorite chair and sipped . . .

***

The three gentlemen sat at a table in the bar of the Napoleon House, still clad in their finery, each holding a glass of wine.

"That was a fine event tonight," Charles Beaumarchette said. "A shame to come away empty handed."

"Did you see them?" Henry Larch asked.

"Who?" Pierre Chambrun asked.

"The Lafittes," Larch said. "The ladies."

"Oh yes," Beaumarchette said, "I saw them. I proposed."

"To which one?" Larch asked. "Mother or daughter?"

"What does it matter?" Chambrun asked. "Either one would do."

"Yes, well," Beaumarchette said, "it doesn't matter, because I proposed to both, and both said no."

"Do you think it's true, what they say about them?" Larch asked.

"You mean about them being related to Jean Lafitte, the pirate?" Chambrun asked.

"Yes," Larch said, "daughter and granddaughter?"

"Who knows?" Chambrun asked. "If you believe in Marie Laveau, you can believe in anything in New Orleans."

"Well," Beaumarchette said, "Marie Laveau is New Orleans royalty, after all."

"And Jean Lafitte?" Chambrun asked. "What is he?"

"A legend," Larch said. "A pirate who helped Andrew Jackson win the Battle of New Orleans."

"A witch and a pirate," Chambrun said. "Both legends in the *Vieux Carre*."

"In more than just the French Quarter," Beaumarchette pointed out. "Also the Bayou."

"And all of New Orleans," Larch said.

"Well," Chambrun said, "if you would marry a Lafitte, would you marry a Laveau?"

"And if either," Beaumarchette asked, "which would it be?"

"Well," Larch said, "considering there's still a fortune in pirate treasure out there, somewhere, I would say Lafitte."

"Then let us raise our glasses to the ladies Lafitte," Beaumarchette said, "and may the best man win."

They all laughed and drank.

***

Marguerite filled her glass a second time, swore it would be the last before bed.

She knew what all the men at the party tonight were thinking. She also knew all the proposals of marriage came to them because of more than their beauty and charm. It was about her father's treasure. Her father had raided many of the Spanish ships in Central America and brought the booty to his island Barataria Bay, Louisiana. And when he had died in 1823, not all of it had been found. The men of New Orleans believed it was out there, somewhere. And they thought that she and Angelique knew where it was. To marry one of them would give a man access to riches, and to their charms.

Marguerite Lafitte considered herself the Queen of the Vieux Carre—though many would have given that title to Marie Laveau and her descendants. But the daughter of a pirate existed, and a witch was just myth.

However, many not only believed in the witch, but feared her. And that was what Marguerite Lafitte wanted for herself and her daughter, to be not only desired, but feared, as well.

Chapter Two

Clint Adams had been to New Orleans on several occasions. But it had been a while and he was looking forward to the unusual things the city had to offer. New Orleans was one of the twenty oldest cities in the country, and possibly the most unique in both culture and architecture.

As he was checking into the Hotel Richelieu, he noticed a party going on in a large room off the lobby. The folks he could see, men and woman meandering, dancing, mixing, were dressed in expensive suits and gowns. And as he completed his check-in, two ladies in lavender gowns came out, collected their wraps from a small check-in room, and headed for the door. They were obviously related, both beautiful, and the older one— probably the mother—looked over at him and smiled before they went out the front door. He didn't even have time to return it.

"Sir?" the clerk said.

He looked and saw the man holding his key out to him.

"Who were those women?" Clint asked. "The ones who just left?"

"Sir, it looked like Marguerite Lafitte, and her daughter, Angelique."

"Laffite?" Clint asked. "Like the pirate?"

"Exactly, sir," the clerk said. "They claim to be Jean Lafitte's daughter and granddaughter."

"Claim?"

"Well," the clerk said, leaning forward and lowering his voice, "just between you and me, sir, I believe they are who they say they are."

"That's interesting," Clint said.

"Anything else, Mr. Adams?"

"I don't think so."

"Is your horse outside?" the clerk asked.

"No, I came in on a riverboat," Clint said. He had left Eclipse in the care of someone he trusted, further up the Mississippi.

"Luggage?"

"Just this," Clint said, picking up a carpetbag from the floor. "I'm good."

"Enjoy your stay, sir."

"I plan to."

The hotel had two floors, and no elevator, which suited Clint since he still couldn't get used to the damned things. Up on the second floor he walked to his room, still aware of the music that was playing downstairs.

Since he intended to stay for at least a week, he unpacked his carpetbag and availed himself of the chest of drawers in the room. He ignored the closet because he really had nothing to hang up. At least, not until he bought a new suit. After all, if he planned to attend festivities like the one going on downstairs at that moment, he would need one.

It was too late in the day to do any shopping, though, and would have to wait until the next day. That left tonight for going down to the street and getting reacquainted with the French Quarter of New Orleans.

***

Any walk on the streets of the French Quarter invariably led to Bourbon Street. The street was alive with lights, music and people. Much of those three things were also up in the balconies and galleries lining the street on both sides.

Many of the men and women were well-dressed, as if they had come from that party at the Richelieu. But this was the way the denizens of New Orleans celebrated, and they usually didn't need any special reason to do it. "Celebrating" was a constant state of being in New Orleans.

Clint walked along Bourbon Street, enjoying the ca-maraderie the festivities seemed to foster. Men laughed and greeted him, offering drinks. Women smiled and waved, pressed up against him, showing off their obvious charms. But Clint had other pressing matters, like the loud grumbling of his stomach and the dryness of his throat.

He stopped into a brilliantly lit saloon called ON THE BAYOU. The interior was jumping with activity, custom-ers spilling in-and-out from the street. He found an opening at the bar and ordered a beer. The bartender served it while hardly looking at him.

Beer in hand he turned, took a healthy swig to lubri-cate his dry throat, and then proceeded to watch the activities in the place.

There was no show going on stage, and no gambling. But the festive mood of New Orleans and the French Quarter needed neither of those things to fuel it. Beautiful girls were working the floor, and even men who already had ladies with them were interacting with them. The Quarter was a place where everyone left their inhibitions not only at the door, but in a drawer at home. He saw customers—male, female and even both going upstairs with another woman. What they would do when they got up there was anybody's guess.

Standing alone, drinking his beer, he was approached by several of the working girls, but he'd been travelling all day and didn't feel the need for female companionship at the moment. And even if he did, he wouldn't pay for it.

He had a second beer, then settled his bill and left, heading out for supper, and a good night's sleep. Tomorrow he would tackle all that the French Quarter had to offer.

Chapter Three

They next day Clint quickly discovered that friends he had known or made during past visits to New Orleans had moved on. So to occupy himself, he moved on to improving his wardrobe by finding clothes more suitable to the French Quarter atmosphere.

He not only bought new suits, but had a tailor make the necessary alterations for a perfect fit. The tailor was a talkative man, so Clint took advantage of that to ask questions.

"How much do you know about French Quarter society, Jacques?"

"Ah, *mon ami*," Jacques said. "I know everything and everyone." Clint didn't know if the man was French, or actually French Creole. His English wasn't perfect, and he tossed out a French phrase every now and then.

"Tell me about the two ladies who claim to be descendants of the pirate, Jean Lafitte."

"Ah," Jacques said, "they are indeed French Quarter society."

"Yes, but are they actually Lafitte's daughter and granddaughter?" Clint asked.

"It is generally accepted that they are," Jacques said.

"By everyone?"

Jacques finished measuring the trousers and stood up. He was a tall, rail-thin man in his forties.

"By most."

"By you?" Clint asked.

"Let us just say I have no reason to doubt them," Jacques said. "When do you want your suits, *mon ami*?"

"Soon as you can finish them, I guess."

"Are you planning to attend some parties in the Quarter?" the tailor asked.

"If I can do it without crashing," Clint said.

"I may be able to help you with both of those things," Jacques said. "I can have the suits ready for you by tomorrow afternoon."

"And the parties?" Clint asked.

"I may have an invitation for you for tomorrow night," Jacques said. "We shall see, eh?"

"Thank you, Jacques," Clint said. "I appreciate it."

***

As Angelique entered the drawing room to join her mother for tea, she saw a man named Adolphe leaving by the patio door.

"Ah, there you are, dear," Marguerite said. "The tea was going to get cold."

"Why was Adolphe here, Mother?" Angelique asked.

They sat on the divan with the tea set-up in front of them on the glass coffee table. Marguerite poured.

"He is doing something for me."

"What?"

"You know that man we saw in the hotel lobby last night?" her mother asked.

"You saw him," Angelique said. "I didn't."

"Well, he interested me," Marguerite said, "so Adolphe is going to find out his identity."

"And then what?"

"I don't know," Marguerite said. "First we have to learn who he is, before I know what I want to do."

"What was it about him that interested you?" Angelique asked.

"Oh, his bearing," Marguerite said. "He stood like a man very confident in himself. I find that very attractive . . . don't you?"

"And he was handsome, right?"

"Oh, yes."

"Mother—"

"For you, my dear," Marguerite said, "I am thinking about him for you."

"I can find my own men, Mother."

"I know you can, my dear," Marguerite said. "We both can. How many marriage proposals did you have last night?"

"One less than you," Angelique pointed out.

"Exactly," Marguerite said, "and none of them were suitable husband material."

"That is for sure," Angelique said, picking up her teacup.

"So we need some new blood," Marguerite said. "And a man who has just arrived in the Vieux Carre qualifies."

"And he is obviously staying at an expensive hotel," Angelique pointed out.

"Yes, he is."

"Mother," Angelique said, "are you looking for a husband for me, or a mark for you?"

"A mark?" Marguerite said. "Where did you learn such a term?"

"What would you call a man you can con some money out of?" Angelique asked.

"We do not con, my dear," Marguerite said. "We loot, the way your grandfather—my father—did."

"Yes," Angelique said, "we are pirates. All we are missing is a ship."

"Drink your tea," her mother said.

Chapter Four

"Your suits are ready," Jacques said, as Clint entered his shop.

"Great!" Clint said.

"You will look splendid in them," the tailor assured him.

"And where will I be looking splendid?" Clint asked.

Jacques reached underneath his counter and came up with a tan envelope.

"You have a party to go to," Jacques said, "tonight."

"That was quick work," Clint said, accepting the invitation. "Who are these folks?"

"It is for a party at the home of Mr. and Mrs. Francois Bouchet." He pronounced the name "Boo-shay." "Monsieur Bouchet is a wealthy financier, while his wife does a lot of charity work."

"And he's a customer?"

"Six suits a month worth," Jacques said. "One of my very best customers."

"Which doesn't explain why he let you invite me to his party," Clint said.

"I told him who you are," Jacques said, "and he insisted I give you an invitation."

"Sounds good," Clint said. He put the invitation in his pocket. "Will I be seeing you there?"

Jacques laughed.

"I am not welcome at such parties," the tailor said. "I am a tailor, a merchant, not part of New Orleans society."

"But you got me invited."

"That I could do," Jacques said. "But attend myself? Unheard of."

"Well . . . what if you went as my guest?" Clint asked.

"That would be embarrassing for all concerned," Jacques said. "Please wait here and I will get your suits."

Clint nodded, and Jacques went into the back of his store.

***

"Who?" Marguerite asked Adolphe.

The bald black man said, "Clint Adams. He is also known as the Gunsmith, him."

"The Gunsmith," she repeated. "Yes, I do know that name."

"He is a very famous gunfighter, dat man," Adolphe said. "Not de kind of man you should be takin' up wit'."

"I don't intend to take up with him, Adolphe," she said. "Don't worry."

"I do worry about you and yours," Adolphe said.

"How's your family and them?" she asked, turning the situation around.

"My maw-maw is poorly," he said, "she got dat cough, but she say she'll be awright."

"I hope she is," Marguerite said. "Give her my best, will you?"

"I do dat, Miss Marguerite, for sure," the black man said, nodding.

"Thank you, Adolphe," she said. "That's all."

"Yes," he said, and withdrew from the room.

A few moments later Angelique came in.

"I saw Adolphe leave, Mama," Angelique said. She saw her mother flinch at being called "Mama," and smiled. "What was his news?"

"The news," Marguerite replied, "is that the Gunsmith is in New Orleans."

"The Gunsmith?"

"The famous gunfighter?"

"I know who the Gunsmith is," Angelique said. "Just tell me what this means to us?"

Marguerite handed her daughter a glass of wine and said, "I have not figured that out yet, but I will."

"So we are going to meet him?"

"We are," Marguerite said. "I know that much."

"When?"

"We'll start with tonight," Marguerite said. "There is a party at the home of Francois Bouchet."

"And what makes you think a western gunfighter will be in attendance?"

"What else would he be doing here?" Marguerite asked, with a shrug.

"Killing someone?" Angelique said. "Isn't that what he does?"

"He will be going to parties," Marguerite said.

"And killing someone there?"

"My dear," Marguerite said, "haven't I taught you that a reputation is not always true?"

"You want people to believe our reputation is true," Angelique pointed out.

"That is because it is true," Marguerite said, heading out of the room.

"Where are you going, Mama?"

"I have to choose a gown for tonight. I suggest you do the same."

Chapter Five

Clint tried the two suits on in his hotel room, chose the one he would wear that night. He opened the envelope and looked at the invitation.

YOU ARE CORDIALLY INVITED TO THE HOME OF MR. AND MRS. FRANCOIS BOUCHET FOR DINNER AND FESTIVITES . . .

He stopped reading after the address. It was definitely a French Quarter location. He wondered what the "festivities" were going to be?

***

Eloise Bouchet turned from the mirror as her husband entered the room.

"Is that what you are wearing tonight?" she asked him.

He looked down.

"What is wrong with my suit?" he asked.

"It's fitted too tight," she said, turning back to the mirror.

"In case you haven't noticed my love," the large, overweight man said, "all my suits are tight, but luckily you still have the kind of body that will distract people from looking at me, especially in a gown like that."

"Like what?" she demanded. "What's wrong with this gown?"

He was going to say it was cut too low, but knew that would only get him into trouble, so instead he said, "It's powder blue. You know I hate powder blue."

"It brings out my eyes," she said.

"Yes, it does," he said, giving in. "and they're love-ly."

She started to fiddle with her auburn hair, even though it looked perfect to him. A man of sixty, he enjoyed having a wife who was almost twenty years younger.

"Did you invite that man?"

"Which man?"

"You know," she said, "the one Jacques told you about."

"Clint Adams!" Bouchet snapped. "Yes, yes, of course I invited him. The man's a legend of the West."

"And you think he'll fit in with our guests?"

Bouchet laughed out loud.

"I don't think he will, at all," he said. "That's what makes him the perfect guest."

She turned and looked at him.

"You're just trying to start trouble, then."

"Not trouble," he said. "I just like to create ripples in the water and see what happens."

"Is the food here?" she asked. "I told Henri to get it here by three."

"I'll go down and check, my love," he said.

"And don't come back up," she said. "You know I need to be alone to get ready."

"You look pretty ready to me," he said.

"Oh God," she said, "I'm hours from ready."

"Then I'll leave you to it."

As he headed for the door she shouted, "Just see to the food!"

***

Clint got into the suit he chose for the night and went down to the lobby. It was five in the afternoon, and he wasn't due at the party until six. But since he didn't want to be one of the first to arrive, he decided not to go until seven. That gave him two hours to kill.

He left the hotel and started walking Chartres Street. He walked to Jackson Square, where vendors did a brisk business among the more traditional shops and restaurants.

He strolled the square, bought a piece of fruit and ate it while watching some the artists ply their trade. One of them was painting a still life of the St. Louis Cathedral, across the way.

"That's very good," Clint said.

"Are you an artist?" the unkempt man asked.

"Well, no—"

"A critic, then?"

"No," Clint said, "just someone who—"

"Then you don't know anything," the artist snapped. "Move along!"

Clint decided to do as the man said. He knew artists tended to be temperamental. The man had not even looked up at him, but kept his eyes either on the cathedral, or his canvas.

He saw some other artists, but decided not to risk their wrath, then left Jackson Square and began looking for a horse drawn cab to take him to the party. By the time he arrived, it should have already been underway.

As the cab took him to his destination, he realized it was just outside the Quarter, on Magazine Street. The large four-columned porch was well lit, announcing not only its majestic presence, but aesthetic, as well.

He paid the driver and headed up the drive to the party.

Chapter Six

Clint was stopped at the door by a tall man wearing a tuxedo.

"Invitation, sir?"

Clint showed it to him.

"Thank you, sir," the man said, not relieving him of it. "Enjoy the evening."

"Thank you," Clint said, pocketing the invitation once again.

As he entered the house, a waiter approached him right in the entry hall, at the base of a staircase, carrying a tray of glasses.

"Champagne, sir?"

"Sure, why not?" Clint said, and took one.

He walked further into the house, where guests were mingling. The men wore expensive suits, the women dazzling gowns. A couple of beautiful women, though they were standing with men, brazenly looking him over with interest.

Clint had reluctantly left his gunbelt in his hotel room, but he had his Colt New Line tucked into his belt at the small of his back. He wondered what the man who had stopped him at the door would have done if he knew.

He had no idea who his host was, beyond the name Francois Bouchet. He started playing a game with himself, trying to pick his host out of the crowd.

"You look lost."

He turned toward the voice, saw a beautiful, auburn haired woman of about forty, wearing a powder blue dress that showed off her bountiful body. She had large breasts, wide hips, and beautiful, smooth skin that spilled out over the décolletage.

"I am," he said. "I'm a stranger here."

"Are you invited?" she asked. "Or are you an interloper?"

"Oh, I have an invitation," he said, starting to go into his pocket.

"I don't need to see it," she said. "I'll take your word for it." She put her hand out. "Eloise. You can call me Ellie."

"Clint," he said, shaking her hand.

The waiter came by again, taking Clint's empty glass and allowing each of them to take another full one.

"What about you?" he asked. "Stranger?"

"Oh," she said, "I've been here before. I can show you around, if you like?"

"I've been trying to figure out who our host is."

"That's easy," she said. "See the fat man over there? In the purple suit and frilly cuffs? That's him."

"Really?" he asked. "That's quite a suit."

"Made especially for him," she said.

"By Jacques?" he asked.

"You know Jacques?"

"He made this suit," Clint said, "though it's not as . . . flamboyant as that one."

"It fits you very well," she said. "Would you like to see the rest of the house?"

"Could we get away with that?" he asked.

"Oh yes," she said. "Like I said, I've been here before. Let me show it to you, and then I'll introduce you to our host."

"Suits me," he said. "Lead the way."

"Let's do the upstairs," she said. "Down here it's all available to the guests."

She took him back to the entry hall and up the stairs. Some of the guests watched them go, but then turned back to their conversations.

"This is quite a house," Clint said.

"Yes," she said, "it has eight bedrooms."

"Eight?"

"Yes," she said, passing one, "this is the master."

He glanced into it as they passed, saw a huge bed covered with pillows.

"And here," she said, waving one hand, "are guest rooms."

"Are there usually any guests here?" he asked.

"Never," she said. "These rooms haven't even been used. Neither have the beds."

She entered one, walked to the bed and sat on it.

"It's very comfortable," she said. "Come and sit."

He walked over and sat next to her. They sipped their champagne. Up close he could feel the heat emanating from her body.

"See?" she said. "Comfortable."

"Yes, it is," he said.

She turned her head to look at him, wet her lips with her tongue, then leaned over and kissed him.

"I'm sorry," she said. "Was that too forward?"

"Not at all," he said. "I've been thinking about doing that since the moment we met."

"Well, then," she said, sliding her free hand into his lap, "perhaps you'll find this too forward."

She rubbed him through his trousers with her hot hand, and his cock began to swell beneath her hand.

"No," he said, "I think that'll be fine."

"How about this?"

She got down on her knees, set aside her glass, undid his trousers, reached in for his cock, pulled it out and engulfed it in her hot mouth.

"That's . . . perfect!" he said.

Chapter Seven

Ellie sucked Clint until he thought the top of his head would blow off, then stood and removed her gown.

"Don't you think we should close the door?" he asked.

"Why?" she asked, her hands behind her as she undid her dress, "don't you think it's exciting thinking we might get caught."

Her gown hit the floor and she stepped out of it. She was fully naked underneath, which led him to think that maybe sex at a moment's notice was a plan of hers.

"Do you do this a lot?" he asked.

"Enough to know that I do it right," she said. "Now let's get you undressed."

She helped him off with his boots, then undid his trousers and slid them down. She divested him of his underwear and his hard cock sprang into view. She started to unbutton his shirt, and noticed he had a gun in his hand.

"Where did that come from?" she asked.

"It was in my belt," he said.

"Do you plan on making love to me at gunpoint?" she asked.

"No," he said, "but I'll be keeping it close."

"So if someone does catch us," she said, "you'll shoot them?"

"That depends," Clint said, "on whether or not they start shooting first."

She took off his shirt, tossed it aside and started rubbing his chest with her hands. He laid the gun aside on the bed and allowed his hands to roam over her body. Her pendulous breasts were topped by luscious brown nipples. He lifted them to his mouth to taste and she groaned as he rolled them between his teeth.

Abruptly, she pushed him down onto his back, mounted him and allowed her breasts to dangle in his face, so he could continue to nip at them. At the same time, she rubbed her pubic patch up and down his cock so he could enjoy the hairy message. Eventually, she reached down to hold him so his penis poked through the forest and entered her hot, wet pussy.

"Oh. God," she groaned, as she sat down on him, taking him all the way in.

As she began to move up and down on him, he forgot about the open door. If someone were to come by and catch them, so be it. Hopefully, they'd have the sense to turn around and walk the other way.

She sat up straight so he could watch her full breasts bob up and down as she bounced on him. The thing that amazed him was that, while he was grunting each time she came down on him, she was completely quiet. He had never been with a woman who didn't make a sound during sex.

Abruptly, she leaned down, placed her hands flat on his abdomen and rather than bounce on him, began to grind. He saw the veins in her neck as she continued to fight the urge to cry out. Suddenly, she stiffened, her eyes went wide, and even as she was going over the edge, she remained silent.

In the next moment he exploded inside of her, and almost pulled a muscle as he tried to match her silence . . .

***

While they dressed quickly she said, "It's been very nice meeting you, Mr. . . ."

"Adams," he said. "Just call me Clint. And you're Ellie—"

Suddenly, she turned, headed for the door and said, "I'll see you downstairs."

"You were going to introduce me to our host," he reminded her.

She stopped at the door and said, "As soon as you come down."

She headed off down the hall and, apparently, back to the party.

Clint pulled his boots on, retrieved his gun from the bed and tucked it into his belt, then put on his jacket. Ellie had gotten her dress on in record time, perhaps because she had experience with open door dalliances like this one.

Clint left the room and walked down the hall to the staircase. He started down the stairs, drawing the attention of the few people who were in the entry hall. He smiled at them as he got to the bottom and grabbed a champagne glass from a passing waiter.

He carried the drink back to the party, looked around for Ellie so he could get that introduction to the host. When he spotted her she was actually coming toward him with a smile on her face.

"Are you ready to meet our host?" she asked.

"Mr. Bouchet? More than ready."

She put her arm through his and guided him across the floor toward the man in the purple suit. When he saw them approaching, he turned to face them, and smiled.

"Francois Bouchet," she said, sliding her arm from Clint's, "meet Clint Adams."

She stepped next to Bouchet and slid her arm through his.

"Mr. Adams," she said, "meet Francois Bouchet—your host, and my husband."

Chapter Eight

Francois Bouchet extended his pudgy hand to shake Clint's, while Ellie gave him an amused look.

"A pleasure to meet the famous Gunsmith," Bouchet said, as they shook hands.

"Thank you for the invitation, Mr. Bouchet," Clint said.

"Oh please," Bouchet said, "you can call me Frankie."

"Frankie?"

"I like it," Bouchet said, "It's so simple, no?"

"Yes," Clint said, "very simple. Like Ellie."

"Ah, yes," Bouchet said, "my Eloise. I should have known she would introduce herself to you." He put his arm around her and kissed her cheek. "She is the perfect hostess."

"She is that," Clint agreed.

"What do you think of our little soiree?" Bouchet asked.

"It's very impressive," Clint said. "Are all these people your friends?"

"Some are friends," he said, "others—like you—are acquaintances, but most of them are hangers-on and moochers, looking for free drinks and free food."

"I see."

"Of course, you are counted in the acquaintance category now, but I hope that soon we will be friends."

"That would be wonderful," Ellie said, still looking amused.

"I hope so, too," Clint said.

"Darling," Ellie said to Bouchet, "there's Rene. You've been wanting to talk with him."

"So I have. Mr. Adams, I'm sorry—"

"I'll see to Mr. Adams, dear," Ellie said. "Go."

"I'm sorry," Bouchet said to Clint, and walked away to talk with "Rene."

"Who's Rene?" Clint asked Ellie.

"A member of the local aristocracy," Ellie said. "Rene DuVal is part of one of the oldest families in New Orleans."

She slid her arm into his again and said, "Let's stroll."

They began to move around the room, with Ellie exchanging greetings with the guests.

"Why didn't you tell me you were my host's wife?" Clint asked.

"Would you have gone upstairs with me if I had?"

"No."

"Then that answers your question."

"So you knew who I was when you, uh, invited me?" he asked.

"We heard from Jacques that you were in New Orleans, and we thought you would be a fine addition to our guest list."

"And?"

She held his arm tightly.

"And I thought you'd be interesting—and you were."

"Interesting."

"Among other things."

At that point, there seemed to be some disturbance near the front of the room.

"What's going on there?" Clint wondered.

"Looks like the ladies have arrived," Ellie said.

"Ladies?"

"The pirate ladies," she said. "I wasn't sure they were going to show up."

"Oh, you mean those women who claim to be related to Jean Laffite?"

"Exactly," she said. "His daughter, and granddaughter."

"And you believe they *are* related?"

"Most everyone in this city who says they're related to someone from our legendary past is telling the truth," she said. "It's like the descendants of Marie Laveau?"

"The witch?"

"Yes," Ellie said. "She has a lot of descendants here about, so why not Jean Laffite? Come on, I should greet them. I'll introduce you."

"Sounds interesting," he said.

"Oh, they're going to like you," she said.

They walked together to the front of the room, where people were pointing and talking among themselves. But Clint noticed that no one was approaching the two women.

He'd noticed the night before how much they looked alike, almost like sisters. Up close, however, he could see that they were obviously mother and daughter, although both of them were beautiful. They had the same full figures, the same jet black hair, although the mother's was shot with a little bit of grey. Both women were showing a healthy expanse of skin. Both were breathtaking.

"Marguerite," Ellie said, as they approached.

"Eloise," the older woman said.

Ellie released Clint's arm and the two women leaned into almost kiss.

"Welcome," Ellie said. "And Angelique."

They did the same lean in, kissing the air on both sides of the other's face.

"Mrs. Bouchet," Angelique said, although she was looking at Clint.

"Ladies, this is Mr. Clint Adams," Ellie said. "He's only just arrived in New Orleans, and we invited him to our little soiree."

"Only you would call this a little soiree, Ellie," Marguerite Laffite said. "Mr. Adams, I think we noticed each other last night."

"Last night?" Ellie asked.

"I was checking into the Hotel Richelieu," Clint said. "How could I not notice two such beautiful ladies."

"How sweet," Angelique said.

"Would you ladies like some champagne?" Clint asked. "It would be my pleasure to get it for you."

"We'd love some," Marguerite said. "Thank you."

Clint went across the room to grab three glasses from a roving waiter's tray. When he returned, the women had their heads together and were laughing. He wondered just what Ellie Bouchet was telling the Laffite ladies?

Chapter Nine

"Here you go," he said, handing each woman a glass.

"Thank you, sir," Ellie said. "Clint, I have to keep mingling. Would you spend some time with these ladies. Nobody else seems to want to."

"It'll be my pleasure."

Ellie walked away and Clint snagged another glass from a passing waiter.

"So," he said, "why not?"

"Why not what?" Marguerite asked.

"Why doesn't anyone come over and talk to you two?"

"That's easy," Angelique said. "They're afraid of us."

Clint looked at Marguerite.

"It's true," she said. "We're Laffites. They're as afraid of us as they are of Marie Laveau and her clan."

"Isn't Marie Laveau dead?" Clint asked.

"The original, yes," Marguerite said, "she's supposed to have died some years back."

"How old was she?" Clint asked.

"Eighty, eighty-one, something like that," Marguerite said.

"Or a hundred-and-eighty," Angelique said. "Mother was actually friends with her."

Clint looked at Marguerite, who didn't look anywhere near a hundred and eighty.

"Some of her family claim she was a lot older than she admitted," Marguerite said, "but then, aren't we all?"

"I'm going to walk around, mother," Angelique said. "See if I can't make some of the women worry about their men. Why don't you keep Mr. Adams company?"

"Just don't get into trouble, dear," Marguerite said.

"Do I ever?"

As Angelique strolled away, swishing her hips, Marguerite said to Clint, "She always gets into trouble. She's a headstrong girl."

"She's very beautiful," Clint said.

"Yes, she is."

"Like mother, like daughter," Clint added.

Marguerite smiled.

"You should have seen me when I was that age," she said. "Men were falling at my feet."

"I'm sure they still are," Clint said.

"You're very gallant," she said. "Come, perhaps we should stroll, as well. Do you mind?"

"Not at all," he said, extending his arm so she could link hers with him.

"I understood that men who made their way with a gun were never without one," she commented.

"Oh, I have one."

"On you?" she asked.

"Yes."

"How exciting," she said. "To think that I might actually get to see you in action."

"Only if your daughter causes that much trouble," Clint told her.

"We'll just have to wait and see, won't we?" she asked, pressing close to him.

***

As they strolled the party, Clint noticed that they were attracting a lot of attention. He put that down to the fact that he was with Marguerite Laffite, not that she was with him. Unless Ellie had spread the word about who he was. Then it might have been the combination of both.

"Oh my," Marguerite said.

"What is it?" Clint asked.

"I see two men who have proposed marriage to my Angelique," she said.

"So trouble is brewing?"

"Indeed."

"The violent kind?"

"The kind that spawns duels," she said.

"Ah, a fair fight," Clint said. "That would be interesting. Swords or pistols?"

"That would depend on who proposes the duel," Marguerite said. "But I think we should find Angelique before they do."

"I think I see her across the room," Clint said.

"Ah, there she is. Would you escort me over to her?"

"Of course."

"And whatever happens here tonight," she said, as they crossed the room, "would you come to my home in the Garden District tomorrow for lunch? I should like to talk to you in a more private setting."

"It would be my pleasure."

They had almost reached Angelique, who was surrounded by several men at that moment, when two other men reached her, coming from different directions.

"Ah, I see it is too late," Marguerite said.

"So what do we do now?" Clint asked.

Marguerite stopped walking and said, "I'm afraid all we can do now is watch."

Chapter Ten

The two men reached Angelique, and both began to speak to her. The other men who had been there backed away.

"So who are they?" Clint asked.

"The one on the right is Andre Jourdan," she said, pronouncing the last name *Joor-dahn*. He is a wealthy bachelor and, as you can see, a very handsome one."

"I see that," Clint said. The man was tall, smooth-faced, probably in his late twenties. "And the other?"

"Louis Vidoq," she said, pronouncing it *Louie Vee-dock*. "Older, as you can see, in his forties, also a bachelor, and also very wealthy. He is from an older New Orleans family."

"And which one does Angelique favor?" Clint asked. "The younger?"

"Neither," Marguerite said. "She has turned them both down many times, but they continue to come back."

"What's wrong with them?" he asked.

"I'm afraid she does not see either as proper husband material," Marguerite said.

"Does she have someone else in mind?" Clint asked.

"Not at the moment."

"So which of these two gentlemen is the swordsman and which favors the pistols?" Clint asked.

"The young Andre is adept with a blade, while Louis prefers the pistol," Marguerite said. "We must wait and see which of them employs his glove, first."

The two men had started to speak to Angelique but were now talking to each other. As their voices grew louder, Angelique—standing between them—looked over at her mother and smiled.

"Oh, you see that smile," Marguerite said. "That smile truly means trouble."

As the two men continued to argue, Angelique re-mained silent, an amused look on her face.

Ellie Bouchet appeared next to Clint and spoke to Marguerite.

"Can you do something?" she asked.

"I could take her home," Marguerite said, "but would that stop those two?"

"Probably not," Ellie said.

And at that point the younger man, Andre, produced a glove and slapped Louis across the face with it.

"Here we go," Marguerite said.

Louis stuck his finger in Andre's face and told him his challenge was accepted. Andre said the weapons would be rapiers.

"I'll see you at first light!" Louis said to Andre.

"Be there with your second!" Andre shouted.

Both men stormed away, leaving Angelique alone. She looked at her mother, shrugged and walked over to where Clint was standing with Marguerite and Ellie.

"Are you happy, now?" her mother asked.

"I think I'm done here, mother," Angelique said. "Can we go?"

Marguerite looked at Ellie.

"You better go," Ellie said, "before she causes another duel."

"What about you, Mr. Adams?" Angelique asked, giving him a coy look. "You'd fight a duel over me, wouldn't you?"

"I'm afraid dueling is not my style," Clint said.

"Good-night, Ellie," Marguerite said. "Thank you for the party."

"Thank you for coming," Ellie said.

She looked at Clint.

"Lunch tomorrow?"

"I'll be there," Clint promised.

"Oh goody," Angelique said. "A dangerous gunman coming to lunch."

"Let's go, my dear," Marguerite said, taking her daughter's arm.

"You're going to Marguerite's for lunch tomorrow?" Ellie asked.

"Yes," Clint said. "She invited me."

"What's it about?"

"She didn't say," Clint answered. "She just said she wanted to talk to me in private."

"You know," Ellie said, "some people believe that Marguerite and Angelique are pirates. It's in their blood."

"Pirates?" Clint said. "Do they have a ship?"

"No one knows," Ellie said. "But some people think they do their pirate looting on land."

"That's interesting," Clint said.

At that moment the man in the purple suit came over and put his arm around his wife.

"Monopolizing my wife, Mr. Adams?"

"You should call me Clint if we're going to be friends," Clint pointed out.

"Clint it is, then," Bouchet said.

"Marguerite is gone?" Bouchet asked his wife.

"Oh yes," she said, "Angelique inspired a duel, and they left."

"Louis and Andre?"

"Yes."

"Are they going to go through with it?"

"Looks like it," Ellie said. "Andre chose the weapons."

"Ah," Bouchet said, "rapiers. I want to see that." He looked at Clint. "Have you ever seen a duel fought with swords?"

"I saw some action with sabers during the war," Clint said, "but I'm not even sure I know what a rapier is."

"It's a long, thin, pointed sword that's usually used for thrusting," Bouchet said. "Andre is quite the expert, so I expect he'll kill Louis."

"Is there any way to stop it?" Clint asked.

"A duel? No, usually the only thing that stops it is when one man dies."

"Where's this duel going to be fought?" Clint asked. "I think I'd like to watch."

"Excellent!" Bouchet said. "I'll pick you up in my carriage, and then after the duel's over, we'll have breakfast. How does that sound?"

"Like a plan," Clint admitted. "Thank you for the offer, Frankie."

"Men," Ellie said, shaking her head. "I don't know why you like to watch men kill each other."

"It's the sport of it, dear," Bouchet said. "Oh, I see somebody else I just have to talk to. See you in the morning, Clint."

As Bouchet walked away Ellie once again linked her arm in Clint's.

"You can see me to the door," he said.

"Are you leaving?" she asked.

"Yes, it's time."

They walked through the entry hall to the front door, where she stopped him.

"We, uh, could go upstairs again," she said, when he opened the door.

"I don't think I'd be able to take the suspense again," he replied.

"You're funny," she laughed. "Are you really going to watch the duel tomorrow with Francois?"

"Yes, I am," Clint said. "It sounds very interesting."

"And then have breakfast together?"

"Yes."

"You're, uh, not going to mention anything . . ."

"Of course not," Clint said. "Do you think I want your husband calling me out for a duel?"

"Now that would be interesting," she said. "He's very good with a pistol at ten paces, you know."

"No," Clint said, "I didn't know."

Chapter Eleven

Clint had met three lovely women at the party. The smell of Ellie Bouchet stayed with him as he went to bed in his hotel, but so did the lovely faces and forms of Marguerite and Angelique Laffite.

He was fascinated by the possibility that they might actually be related to the famed pirate. But as he woke the next morning, he was more interested in the duel that was scheduled to take place.

As he stepped through the front door of the hotel, a carriage drawn by two horses pulled up and the back door swung open.

"Just in time!" Francois Bouchet said, sticking his head out. "Let's go!"

Clint acknowledged the driver with a nod before getting into the back with Bouchet. Today, the man was again clad in lavender, another suit undoubtedly from Jacques.

"Sleep well?" Bouchet asked.

"Yes, thanks."

"Good, good," Bouchet said. "I'm afraid this won't be very interesting for you. Your preference runs to guns, doesn't it?"

"I'm very interested in this sword duel," Clint said.

"Well, it'll be over fairly quickly," Bouchet predicted. "Andre is a master swordsman. Louis won't have a chance."

"So he knows Andre will kill him?"

"Undoubtedly."

"And he'll still show up?"

"He must," Bouchet said. "Or he'll be shamed."

"Wouldn't he rather be shamed than dead?" Clint asked.

"Would you?" Bouchet asked. "If you were challenged?"

"I've been challenged many times," Clint said.

"And each time you put in an appearance," Bouchet said.

"Yes."

"Because if you didn't, the word would have gotten around that you, the Gunsmith, were frightened. And then even more challengers would appear. Isn't that right?"

"It is."

"Then you understand, don't you?"

"Actually, I do," Clint said. "But is this legal in New Orleans?"

"It's illegal everywhere," Bouchet said. "The last legal duel took place in eighteen fifty-nine between two political opponents in San Francisco."

"But they're still fought here, in the South?"

"Oh yes," Bouchet said. "They just have to be kept quiet."

"Who else knows about this one?" Clint asked.

"Everybody who was at the party."

"And there were no lawmen there last night?" Clint asked.

"Oh, heavens, no," Bouchet said. "We do not invite the law to our parties. Who knows what will occur there."

Who knew, indeed, Clint thought, thinking back to Ellie Bouchet.

When the carriage stopped and they got out, Clint saw that they were in a field. In the distance were trees and water.

"The bayou," Bouchet said, getting out behind him. "Best place for a duel to go unnoticed by the law."

Nearby, Clint saw a man waving at the air with a sword.

"That's Andre," Bouchet said. "It figures he would be the first one here."

Clint thought the younger man looked very graceful.

"Maybe Vidoq won't show, after all," Clint said.

"He will be here," Bouchet said. "You may count on that."

While they watched another carriage, drawn by a single horse, pulled to a stop next to theirs. The back door opened, and a man Clint recognized as Louis Vidoq got out. He had another man with him, his second.

The second held a case out to Vidoq, who opened it and took out a rapier. He began slashing at the air.

Clint looked around, saw that he and Bouchet were the only spectators there, other than the two duelists, and their seconds.

"I thought there'd be more people here to watch," he commented.

"They don't need that many witnesses," Bouchet said. "We will do."

As Vidoq began to walk toward Jourdan, Clint and Bouchet followed.

"The two seconds are actually the only witnesses they need," Bouchet said. "We are just extras."

"Who are the seconds?" Clint asked.

"Jourdan's is his brother-in-law, Pierre Martine," Bouchet said. "Vidoq's is his attorney, Ralph Conrad."

"An attorney?" Clint asked. "At an illegal duel?"

"He's been the family attorney for many years," Bouchet said, as if that explained it all.

Clint suddenly wondered if he was going to witness a murder, not a duel.

"Maybe we should stop this," he suggested. "I mean, if we're sure Jourdan's going to kill Vidoq."

"Well," Bouchet said, "anything could happen. Louis might be a better swordsman than anyone thinks. Andre might trip over his own feet and fall on Louis' blade."

"But I—"

"You could not stop them if you tried, Clint," Bouchet said. "They would just come back another day, when you are not here."

"So we have no choice but to watch."

Bouchet shrugged and said, "We are here."

Chapter Twelve

As they watched, the two men crossed swords, and then began. The sound of steel striking steel echoed through the bayou.

It didn't end as quickly as it had begun.

"They look evenly matched," Clint commented.

"I believe," Bouchet said, "that Andre is toying with him."

"So the reason for this duel is Angelique?" Clint asked.

"That is usually the cause of a duel here in New Orleans," Bouchet said. "A woman. And a woman such as Angelique, well she causes many duels."

"This has happened before?"

"Many times," Bouchet said. "Two men propose to her, and then must settle it between them."

"And the winner expects to marry her?"

"Yes," Bouchet said, "he expects it, but it does not happen."

"Then what?" Clint asked.

"Then he continues to pursue her," Bouchet said. "And when another man enters the scene—*voila*! Another duel."

"What does her mother think of all this?"

"Marguerite," Bouchet said, "is the only woman in New Orleans to have more duels fought over her than Angelique."

"I suppose I can see that," Clint said, "in both cases."

A cry of pain attracted their attention, and a flash of red on the arm of Louis Vidoq.

"First blood," Bouchet said. "Now it begins in earnest."

"What were they doing up to now?" Clint asked.

"Feeling each other out," Bouchet said. "Looking for weaknesses."

"But you said Andre was toying with him."

"Yes," Bouchet said, "watch."

They went back and forth for a few more moments, and then there was a flash of blood on Vidoq's other arm.

"What's he doing?" Clint asked.

"He wants to humiliate him," Bouchet said. "But he also wants to give Louis the opportunity to yield."

"And if he does?"

"Then he will live, but in shame."

"And do you think Vidoq will go for that?"

Bouchet laughed shortly and said, "No."

"And as a member of one of New Orleans' oldest families, what would *they* think?"

"They'd be ashamed and shun him."

"That's kind of harsh, isn't it?" Clint asked.

"That's New Orleans' society, Clint," Bouchet explained.

At that moment Andre Jourdan lunged. Louis Vidoq dropped his sword, grabbed his belly, staggered around, and then fell to the ground and lay still.

Francois Bouchet turned to Clint and said, "Breakfast?"

***

Bouchet had the driver take them to a restaurant on Bourbon Street called Café Remoulade. They greeted the man as if they had been waiting for him forever.

"Your table is ready, Monsieur Bouchet."

"Thank you, Henri."

They followed the tuxedoed Henri to the table, and the man said, "Set for two, as you requested."

"Thank you, Henri. This is my friend, Monsieur Adams."

"A pleasure," Henri said, with a short bow. "Pierre will be with you shortly."

"We are in no rush, Henri," Bouchet said. "Just start us off with some of your excellent coffee."

"Oui, Monsieur," Henri said. "Very black, and strong?"

"Wonderful!" Bouchet said.

"You eat here a lot," Clint commented.

"Not as much as I would like, but yes," Bouchet said. "Whenever I can."

"With or without your wife?"

"Preferably without."

Clint gave the man a look.

"Eloise eats like a bird," Bouchet explained, "and frowns at me while I eat. It is a most unpleasant way to spend a meal."

"I imagine it would be."

"Would you like me to order for both of us?" Bouchet said. "It will be nothing too fancy, I assure you."

"By all means," Clint said, "order whatever you like, I'm sure it'll be great."

"Oh," Bouchet said, "of that you can be sure."

Chapter Thirteen

Frankie Bouchet ordered two andouille sausage Cajun scrambles.

"Eggs and sausage," he told Clint, "Cajun style."

"If it's as good as this coffee," Clint said, "that's all I can ask."

"So what did you think of the duel?" Bouchet asked, stirring four sugar cubes into his coffee.

"I'm not sure," Clint said. "It was interesting, but I'm not sure I didn't just stand by and watch a murder."

"Anywhere other than New Orleans, and you might call it that," Bouchet said. "But no one here would."

"Not even the law?"

"The law will not find out about it."

"What about Vidoq's body?" Clint asked.

"The family will take care of that," Bouchet said. "The police will never even see it."

Clint fell silent, drank his coffee.

"You don't intend to go to the law, do you, Clint?" Bouchet asked.

"No," Clint said, "not at all. Hey, I said I wanted to watch, and I did. If I report it, I might be in as much trouble as anyone."

"That's true."

"So there you are," Clint said. "We're all in the same boat."

The waiter, Pierre, came with their plates, and the aroma set Clint's stomach to growling. He served the eggs and andouille sausage with biscuits, and when Clint took the first bite, the spices exploded in his mouth.

They suspended their conversation while they ate.

***

"That was delicious," Clint said, while Pierre cleared the plates away.

"Yes, it was," Bouchet said. He sat back and rubbed his big belly. "I'm tempted to have another order. Do you mind?"

"Go ahead," Clint said. "I'll have some more of this great coffee while you eat." Clint leaned forward. "And I won't frown at you."

Bouchet smiled and waved, and Pierre brought over the second order. Apparently, this was what Bouchet usually did, and the waiter was ready.

"Besides," Clint went on, "I can't eat more. I'm supposed to have lunch with Marguerite."

"That's right," Bouchet said, around a mouthful of andouille. "You're seeing the lovely Laffite ladies today."

"Well," Clint said, "one of them."

"Oh, don't worry," Bouchet said. "Little Angelique will be there. She would never just let her mother have a man all to herself. Those two are very competitive."

"For Marguerite to be a daughter of Jean Laffite," Clint said. "she'd have to be . . . what? Sixty?"

"About that."

"She doesn't look a day over forty," Clint said.

"And all the men in New Orleans know it."

"And Angelique?" Clint asked.

"In her twenties."

"So Marguerite had her a bit late in life, didn't she?" Clint asked.

"I suppose."

"And who was the father?"

"No one knows."

"Any other children?"

"No, there's just the two of them."

"And are they wealthy?"

"Are you looking for a rich wife?" Bouchet asked.

"I'm not looking for any kind of wife," Clint said. "I'm just curious."

"Some folks think they're richer than others," Bouchet said. "Jean Laffite was supposed to have left a fortune in booty."

"And they have it?"

"If they've found it," Bouchet said. "He hid it."

Clint had fairly recently been involved with another pirate's treasure, that one belonging to Blackbeard. He had no desire to search for another one.

"Are they well off without the treasure?"

"Oh yes," Bouchet said, "they're not suffering. There are plenty of wealthy men in New Orleans trying to buy their hearts—or, at least, their charms."

"I wonder what Marguerite wants with me?"

"She's probably impressed by you," Bouchet said. "After all, her father was a legend, and so are you."

"You think that's it?"

"How often does a woman have a chance to have tea, or lunch, with a legend?" Bouchet asked. "As a matter of fact, why don't' you come to the house for supper tonight?"

"I'd be getting all my meals for free today," Clint commented.

"It's our pleasure, believe me," Bouchet said. "What do you say? Eloise would love to have you."

Clint thought, she'd already had him, and said, "I'll be there."

Chapter Fourteen

"Do you really think this is a good idea. Mother?" Angelique asked.

"Is what a good idea?"

"Having the Gunsmith here for lunch."

"Why would it not be?" Marguerite asked. "The man is a legend. We're lucky he agreed to come."

"Yes, but why did you invite him?" Angelique asked.

"Well, aside from being a legend of the West, he's a fine looking man, isn't he?"

"Yes, he is," Angelique said. "But he's a little old for me, and a little young for you."

"Bite your tongue, my dear!" Marguerite said. "Watch what you're saying."

"Which comment are you objecting to?" the younger girl asked her mother.

"Both!"

***

Clint took a carriage to the Garden District and was impressed when it pulled up in front of the Laffite home. It was a two story Mansion that looked like something from the pre-Civil War South. There was a lot of land surrounding it, covered with trees, bushes and other foliage. He made his way up the walk and knocked on the front door. It was opened by a tall, young black woman wearing a maid's uniform.

"Suh?"

"Clint Adams," he said. "I've been invited to lunch by . . . Madame Laffite." He wasn't sure what to call her, but came up with "Madame."

"Please, come in." He stepped past her and she closed the door, turned to face him. "Please wait one minute. I'll tell Madam you're here."

Clint had said "Madame" but the maid said "Madam."

He waited in a large entry hall, like the one he'd seen the night before at the Bouchet home. When the maid returned, Marguerite was walking behind her.

"That'll be all, Nina," she said.

"Yes, Ma'am."

"Clint," she said, extending her hand and smiling. "How nice to see you."

He wasn't sure if she wanted him to shake her hand, or kiss it, so he simply held it briefly.

"Thank you for the invitation," he said. "You have a beautiful home, here."

"Come with me," she said. "We're having lunch on the veranda, overlooking the back garden."

"Is it just the two of us?" he asked, as he followed.

She was wearing an expensive looking dress, violet in color, with no skin showing, but it clung to her figure, making walking behind her a very pleasant exercise. She turned her head to speak over her shoulder.

"No, Angelique will be eating with us," she said. "I hope you don't mind."

"Lunch with two beautiful women?" he said. "Why would I object to that?"

"You're very gallant."

She led him out to the veranda, where Angelique was sitting at a glass topped table. On the table was a wooden board of various kinds of meat, all cooked and ready to be consumed. Angelique was wearing a dress similar to her mother's, in blue. The style fit them both. Marguerite was not dressing too young, and Angelique was not dressing too old. The women were so similar, even though they must've been more than thirty years apart in age.

The younger woman said, "Mr. Adams, welcome."

"Please," he said. "Call me Clint."

Angelique didn't extend her hand, so he didn't have to decide whether to shake or kiss it.

"We hope you don't mind a charcuterie board."

He assumed this was the technical name for the board of meats on the table, so he said, "Not at all. It looks delicious."

"Neither of us is familiar with the kitchen," Marguerite said, "and I forgot our cook has the day off, so we brought this in. Please, have a seat."

Next to the board was also a basket, filled with a variety of breads, and two pots, one with coffee, and one with hot water for tea.

Clint waited for the ladies to sit, and then followed.

"Please, help yourself," Marguerite said.

While he constructed a sandwich Angelique asked, "Did you see the duel this morning?"

"I did."

"Can you tell me—us—who won?"

"Is it important to you?" Clint asked.

"The duel was over her, Clint," Marguerite reminded him.

"That's right," Clint said. "I'm afraid Andre toyed with Louis for a while, and then killed him."

"That's a shame," Marguerite said. "His family will be devastated."

"I was given to understand they'd be proud of the way he died," Clint said.

"A duel is a stupid way to die!" Marguerite snapped.

"Mother!"

"I'm afraid my daughter and I have different opinions on the subject," Marguerite said.

"I can see that."

"It's a tradition," Angelique said, "that should not be trivialized."

"Are you speaking about dueling," Clint asked, "or dueling over you?"

Angelique smiled, picked up a piece of meat, shrugged and answered, "Both."

"And you?" Clint asked, looking at Marguerite. "How many duels have been fought over you?"

"A lot," she admitted. "Too many."

"How else will we find the right man?" Angelique asked.

"So the last one standing will be the right one?"

"Perhaps," Angelique said.

"Or there might not be a right one," Marguerite said.

"What about Angelique's father?" Clint asked. "Was he the right one?"

"Oh God, no!" Marguerite said, and both she and her daughter laughed.

"What's the joke?"

"Angelique's father was a handsome, drunken sod," Marguerite said.

"I never knew him," Angelique said.

"Well," Clint said, "obviously you got your looks from your mother."

Marguerite smiled.

Angelique asked, "More coffee?"

"Yes, please."

Chapter Fifteen

"So what's going on?" Clint asked.

"Excuse me?" Marguerite said.

"Why the invitation to lunch, when you hardly know me?" Clint asked.

"Perhaps that's it," Angelique said. "We want to get to know you. After all, we've been told you're a legend."

"You didn't hear that from me," he said.

"So are you saying it's not true?" Marguerite asked.

"No," Clint replied, "just that you didn't hear that from me. And you won't."

"Then you're modest," Marguerite said.

"Or shy," Angelique said.

"Now Jean Laffite," Clint said, "there's a legend. And you're his daughter and granddaughter. That's impressive."

"But why?" Angelique said. "We haven't done anything but be born with his name."

"That's not what I heard," Clint said.

"Well," Marguerite said with a smile, "you haven't heard what you heard from us."

"Touché," he said.

"Do you want anymore?" Marguerite asked.

"No," Clint said, "I've had enough. It was all delicious."

She stood up.

"Let's you and me walk in the garden."

"What about Angelique?" Clint asked, looking at the younger woman. "I don't want to be rude."

"I'll live with it," Angelique said. "Go ahead and walk with mother. I'll see you later."

"You will?"

Angelique smiled.

"Count on it."

Clint looked at Marguerite.

"Looks like I'm all yours, for now," he said, standing.

"That sounds good to me," she said. "This way."

She led him off the veranda, along a stone path until they reached the lush greens, reds, and yellows of the garden. There was also turquoise, magenta and blue.

The stone walk continued on into the flowers, so Clint followed her there.

"You wanted to know why I invited you to lunch," she said. "Do you still want to know?"

"Very much," Clint said.

"Let me see if I can sum it up," she said.

Chapter Sixteen

"I think you could be of great help to me," Marguerite said.

"In what way?"

"With Angelique."

"What's the problem?"

"She's a headstrong girl," Marguerite said. "Actually, I should probably say 'woman,' not girl."

"She certainly seems to like having men duel over her."

"That's only a small part of it," Marguerite said. "She takes after her grandfather."

"The pirate?"

"Indeed. She fancies herself something of a pirate."

"Well now," Clint said, "seems I heard that about both of you."

"Don't get me wrong," Marguerite said, "I'm proud of my heritage. I consider my father a great man. But Angelique is more enamored with his piracy than any of his other achievements."

Clint knew about Jean Lafitte's history in assisting Andrew Jackson win the last battle of the War of 1812.

"Have you ever heard of Barataria Bay?" she asked.

"I haven't."

"It's a group of islands near here. My father was supposed to have a warehouse, from where he disposed of his pirate booty."

"Ah."

"Angelique wants to go there."

"What does she expect to find? Treasure?"

"Not at all," Marguerite said. "She simply wants to see where her grandfather conducted his business."

"And?"

She stopped walking the path, turned to face him.

"And what?" she asked.

"I thought I heard an 'and' in there," he said.

"You're very perceptive. *And* . . . I believe if she finds his warehouse, she may want to start using it."

"For what?"

"The same thing her grandfather used it for."

"Disposing of booty?" Clint asked. "What booty?"

Marguerite shrugged. "But piracy is no longer looked upon as something . . . romantic."

"Was it ever?"

"You would be surprised," she answered. "It was even romanticized by men—young men, that is. But now this young lady, my daughter, still sees the romantic side to it."

"Well," Clint said, "she'd need a ship and a crew. Where would she expect to find that?"

"On the island, I'm afraid."

"Is there only one island there?" he asked.

"That's just it," Marguerite said. "There are many islands. She'll have to find the right one."

"And is she going alone?"

Marguerite turned and started strolling again. Clint followed along.

"She can't go alone," she said.

"Then who's going with her?"

Marguerite looked at him.

"Me?"

"That is what I would like."

"I don't know the first thing about being on a ship," he said.

"That would be no problem," Marguerite said. "Angelique knows everything there is to know."

"Then why would she need me?" Clint asked.

"You've seen the way she is with men," Marguerite said. "That is where she would need help. Dealing with men. That is where you would be helpful."

"What makes you think she won't affect me the way she affects other men?" Clint asked. "What makes you think I won't end up fighting a duel over her?"

She turned to face him but kept walking backward.

"You are not a foolish man," she said.

"You mean I'm not a young man."

"No," She held up her forefinger. "You are not foolish. Louis Vidoq was not a young man, and look what happened to him. He was foolish. Foolishness is not only found in young men." She pointed at him. "But it is not in you."

"You've only known me one day," he said.

"I am an excellent judge of character." She stopped walking. "Come, let's go back to the house."

They walked back quickly through the garden rather than strolling. When they reached the veranda again, Angelique was not there.

"You don't need to decide now," she said. "Think it over. It's a big favor to ask, and you've only known me for one day, also."

"That's true."

"And there's one more thing."

"What's that?"

Marguerite looked around, then leaned in and said, "She must think that it's her idea for you to go with her."

"You think I can convince her of that?"

"I think you must be a very clever man, to have lived this long," she said. "To have lived long enough to become a living legend."

"Should I leave now?" he asked.

"No," Marguerite said, "Angelique will be back down, soon."

"All right."

"Sit," she said. "Have some more coffee."

"Do you think I'll make my decision here, today?" he asked.

"No," she said. "It might help you to talk to her, first."

"All right."

"But don't mention it to her," Marguerite said. "Not the islands, or the piracy. Let her bring it up."

"Then what do I talk about?" he asked.

She smiled.

"I'm sure you'll think of something," she said. "I'll be leaving you alone with my daughter for at least two hours—if you have that much time to give me?"

"It's fine," he said. "I have nothing to do tonight but have supper with the Bouchets."

"Ah," she said, "Ellie. You should watch out for her. She is dangerous."

"I'll keep that in mind."

"I will see you in two hours."

She left the veranda, and he poured himself a cup of coffee.

Chapter Seventeen

He was still working on that cup of coffee when Angelique came back to the veranda. She was still wearing the same simple-but-expensive dress and looked beautiful in it. She also seemed to have run a brush through her long, flowing locks of black hair.

"Where's mother?" she asked.

"I don't really know," he said. "Somewhere in the house, I think."

"She left us alone?"

"Looks like it."

Angelique frowned.

"Why?"

"She didn't say. She just told me to have another cup of coffee."

Angelique sat down across from Clint but didn't touch the coffee or tea pot.

"What did the two of you talk about in the garden?" she asked.

"Lots of things," he said, "but her favorite subject was you."

"Me? What about me?"

"She loves you very much, and she's proud of you," Clint replied.

"I love her, too," Angelique said, "but I have to be my own woman."

"And you do that by having men fight duels over you?" he asked.

"Oh, heavens, no," she said, waving her hand, "that's just for fun."

"Then what do you mean?" he asked, giving her the opportunity.

Angelique leaned her head back and shouted, "Nina!"

The black maid appeared immediately.

"Yes, Miss?"

"A bottle of champagne please, Nina, and two glasses."

"Comin' up, Miss."

"Champagne?" Clint asked.

"Yes," Angelique said, "we're going to celebrate."

"Exactly what are we celebrating?"

"You'll see . . ."

***

Nina brought the bottle, already opened, and Angelique poured two glasses.

"I'm a pirate."

Well, Clint thought, that didn't take long.

"Your grandfather was a pirate," Clint said. "Piracy is a little . . . in the past, isn't it?"

"You would think so," she said, "but no. There are still boats out there, waiting to be plucked."

"I see," Clint said. "And you're going to pluck them?"

"As soon as I get a crew."

"And how do you propose to do that?"

"By proving I'm worth following," she said. "And before you ask how I propose to do that, I'll tell you." She stood up. "But not here."

"Then where?"

"The garden. Did my mother take you to the center?"

"No, we strolled but turned back before we got there," he said.

"Come," she said. "I'll show you."

She started for the steps that led from the veranda to the garden with her glass in hand, but stopped and said over her shoulder, "Bring the bottle, and your glass."

He reached back, grabbed the bottle, and followed her down the steps.

Chapter Eighteen

Angelique didn't stroll, as her mother had. She took long strides across the garden, causing Clint to have to rush to catch up.

"Are we in a hurry?" he asked.

"I don't know how much time mother will give us," she said. "I don't want to be interrupted."

They passed the point where Marguerite had turned around and Clint realized they were in a maze. Angelique obviously knew her way through it, and before long they were in a clearing at the center.

"Nobody will interrupt us here," she said. "I'm the only one who knows the way here."

She sat down on the grass and patted the spot next to her. He sat, and she held out her glass for more champagne. He obliged, then managed to get the bottle to stand on the grass next to him.

"What are we celebrating?" he asked.

"Our partnership," Angelique said, holding her glass out. "Well, come on, you're supposed to clink glasses."

"What makes you think we're partners?"

"Oh, come on," she said. "My mother must've told you about Barataria Bay."

Clint decided to play it straight and not lie to her. Maybe he had already been lied to.

"Yes, she did."

Angelique sipped her champagne.

"She thinks I don't know," she said, "so let's not tell her. Okay?"

"All right."

"She asked you to go with me?"

"Yes."

"You know," she said, "I'm not sure what we'll find there. The United States invaded it in eighteen-fourteen. They may have cleaned it out."

"Does that matter?" he asked. "I thought you just wanted to be able to say you found it."

"That's true enough," she said. "But it would be nice if there was something left."

"Booty? Treasure?"

"Something of my grandfather's," she said. "That would excite me." She ran her fingertips inside the neckline of her dress. "In fact," she said, "I'm getting excited, already."

***

Marguerite came down and found Nina clearing the table on the veranda.

"Where did they go?" she asked.

"The garden, Madame," Nina said.

"Did you hear anything they said?"

"No, Madame," Nina said. "I don't listen."

"Of course not."

"Should I leave this?" Nina asked, indicating the table, which she had only partly cleared.

"No," Marguerite said, "continue."

She left the veranda and went upstairs to her bedroom. Her window overlooked the garden. No one was allowed in her room, so no one had ever seen that view but her, not even Angelique. So her daughter did not know that Marguerite could see everything—even the center of the maze—from there.

She watched, smiling . . .

***

The champagne bottle got knocked over during the sex.

Staring at him, setting her glass aside, she gripped the top of her dress and yanked on it. It came down to her waist, revealing her naked breasts. She had obviously dressed for this. She stood up, pulled the dress off the rest of the way, revealing her nakedness underneath.

She stepped closer to him while he was still seated on the grass, so that her dark pubic patch was right in front of him. He reached out, ran a hand up the back of her right thigh, then around to the front. He probed through the patch of hair with his fingertips, finding her already wet.

She reached for his head with both hands and pulled his face to her. First, he kissed the smooth, pale skin of her belly, then he pressed his face to her patch and probed it with his tongue. She jerked when he licked her, as if she'd been stung, but then she sighed as he continued to taste her juices. She became even wetter as his tongue became more active.

"Oooh," she moaned, as her knees went weak.

He reached behind her, held her tight and lowered her to the grass. Then he got back down between her legs and resumed his licking. Before long she was jerking about, spasms of pleasure wracking her body.

While she calmed herself, he stood and undressed. When he was naked, he started to get down with her, but she put her hands on his thighs to stop him, then got to her knees and took his hard cock in both hands. She fondled it, then pressed it to her face, then rubbed it across her breasts and nipples before finally licking it. When she had it good and wet, she took it into her mouth and began to suck him.

He had both the urge to get up on his toes, and fall flat on his back. Reaching down to cup her head in his hand, he remained standing and closed his eyes, surrendering to the sensations that were running through his body. When he was about to explode into her mouth, she released him and got down onto her back.

"Come on, come on," she gasped, "let us seal this partnership."

"Is that what we're doing?" he asked.

She gave him a hurt look.

"You are going to help me, aren't you, Clint?" she said. "My mother asked you, and now I am. Can you resist us both?"

"At the moment," he said, "I can't resist you."

That made her smile, and when he got down on the grass with her, she laughed. She spread her legs so he could kneel between them, and he drove his hard cock into her wet, steaming depths . . .

***

Still upstairs in her bedroom, watching from her window, Marguerite clapped her hands together.

The partnership was sealed.

She knew she could count on her daughter.

Chapter Nineteen

When Clint and Angelique returned to the veranda from the garden Marguerite was not there.

"Shall I wait to say goodbye to your mother?" he asked.

"I'll say goodbye for you," she promised.

"Then I'll see you tomorrow," Clint said.

"Meet me in Jackson Square, by the cathedral, on the Pirate's Alley side."

"Very fitting," he said.

She smiled.

"I thought so."

He reached out.

"You have some grass in your hair."

He plucked it out. She reached up and took hold of his wrist.

"Thank you."

"Thank your Mother for the lunch," he said, retrieving his hand.

"I will. I'll have Nina show you out. Nina!"

The black maid appeared instantly.

"Show Mr. Adams out, please."

"Yes, Miss."

He followed Nina to the front door, but before she opened it, she turned to face him. Suddenly, she seemed taller, as if she had been slumping to hide her height.

"You must be careful," she said.

"Of what?" he asked.

"These two women," Nina said. "They are dangerous."

"Most women are, Nina."

"I am just warning you, suh," she said. "Be careful."

She opened the door to let him out.

"Thank you, Nina," he said, "but you should know that I'm always careful."

She didn't respond, and he stepped outside. She closed the door firmly behind him.

***

"Well, how did it go?" Marguerite asked her daughter, when she came into the drawing room.

"Mother," Angelique said, "you watched the whole thing. Do you think I don't know your window overlooks the entire garden?"

"Have you been in my room?" her mother demanded.

"No," Angelique said, "but if you can see the garden from your window, then I can see your window from the garden."

"So it went well," Marguerite said.

"It went extremely well," Angelique said. "The Gunsmith lived up to one aspect of his reputation very admirably. But you'll be finding that out for yourself, at some point, won't you?"

"Angelique!" her mother snapped. "At my age?"

"Oh, mother!"

***

Clint went back to his hotel and washed up, then sat on his bed. He checked the Colt New Line to be sure it was still working after lying in the grass for a while. He decided to clean it, and while he did, he thought about the two Lafitte women, Marguerite and Angelique, as well as their maid, Nina. With three people in that house, there was a good chance somebody wasn't telling him the truth. The maid wouldn't have any reason to lie, so she had obviously felt he needed to be warned. Angelique had also seemed to be pretty honest, so he assumed it was the mother who was lying to him.

She had made it seem like Angelique didn't know she was asking Clint to help her. It was more likely the two women had manipulated him into agreeing. But he might have agreed, anyway. Finding Lafitte's island in Barataria Bay sounded pretty interesting.

When he finished cleaning his gun, he realized he was pretty tired from the afternoon's exertions. He decided to take a nap to get himself ready to dine with Francois and Eloise Bouchet.

Chapter Twenty

At the home of the Bouchets, the front door was open not by a maid, but by a butler—a stocky black man wearing a black suit and white gloves.

"Mr. Adams?" he greeted.

"That's right."

"Right this way, sir," the man said. "Mr. and Mrs. Bouchet are waiting for you."

"Am I late?" Clint asked, entering the house.

"Not at all, sir. Follow me, please."

He led Clint across the entry hall, past the staircase and down a hall to a room, with plush furniture, filled with bookshelves.

"Ah, Clint," Francois Bouchet said. "So nice to see you!"

"Frankie," Clint said, looking around.

"Ellie will be down shortly," Bouchet said. "She's making herself beautiful for you."

Clint looked at Bouchet's face, but his expression was completely guileless.

"Drink?" his host asked.

"Sure."

"I have brandy, whiskey—"

"Whisky's good," Clint said. He preferred beer, but he would rather have had whiskey over brandy.

Bouchet poured himself a snifter of brandy, handed Clint a glass, with two fingers of whiskey in it.

"How was your lunch today?" he asked. "With the Lafitte ladies?"

"It was . . . very interesting," Clint said, sipping his drink.

"Did they want anything in particular from you?" Bouchet asked.

"Oh, just some nonsense about wanting to have lunch with a legend, since they are descended from a legend. I didn't really understand it, but the food was good."

"That's all?"

"That's it," Clint said. "They're two lovely women. I might see one or both of them, again."

"And if one," Bouchet asked, grinning, "which one would it be?"

"I don't know . . . yet," Clint said.

"Don't know what?" Ellie asked, coming into the room. Bouchet was right. She had made herself beautiful. She wore a long, floral dress that showed just a hint of cleavage, covering her completely while outlining her shape very nicely.

"Clint was just telling me he didn't know which of the Lafitte ladies he'd like to . . . see again," Bouchet told his wife.

"Does it really matter?" Ellie asked. "They're both cheap tarts."

"Ellie!" Bouchet said.

"May I have a brandy, dear?"

"Yes."

While he poured, Clint said to Ellie, "I thought you and Marguerite were friends?"

"We are," Ellie said, accepting the glass from her husband, "but that doesn't make her less of a tart. Or her daughter. In fact, Angelique is even moreso. Look what she did to poor Louis Vidoq."

"She didn't force him to fight a duel over her," Clint pointed out.

"Didn't she?" Ellie asked. "Her beauty does it."

"Then it's not her fault."

"You're defending her?" Ellie asked.

"No," Clint said, "just stating a fact."

Ellie looked at her husband.

"I'll arrange for dinner to be served," she said. "Ten minutes."

"We'll be there."

Ellie nodded and left, without looking at Clint. He had the distinct feeling she was jealous. But which Lafitte woman was she jealous of?

"I'm sorry. She's a little tense, these days," Bouchet said.

"Do you know why?" Clint asked.

"No," he said. "But that's husbands and wives. We don't know everything about each other. That's what keeps the magic in our relationship."

"I wouldn't know."

"You've never been married?" Bouchet asked.

"No."

"Never wanted to be?"

"Once."

"What happened?"

"She died."

"I'm sorry," Bouchet said. "I didn't mean to bring on bad memories."

"That's okay," Clint said. "They're not so bad. It was a long time ago."

They heard a bell from another part of the house.

"Ah," Bouchet said, "dinner. Shall we?"

"Lead the way," Clint said.

Chapter Twenty-One

Dinner was delicious.

Tense, but delicious.

If Francois Bouchet didn't know why his wife was tense, Clint had a good idea. She wasn't happy that he'd had lunch with the Lafittes. He was surprised the woman would feel jealousy after the short time they had spent together. He'd had the feeling it was something she had done many times before with other men. So why be jealous now?

Francois did most of the talking during dinner, going on about some of the people in town he didn't like. Eloise would roll her eyes occasionally but held her tongue. Clint listened and nodded every so often.

Over dessert, a man wearing a dark suit entered the diningroom and approached Bouchet, handing him a note. He read it, then said to the man, "Yes, all right. I'll be right along."

The man withdrew.

"I'm sorry, Clint," Bouchet said, "but something has come up and I must leave."

"I can go—" Clint started, but Bouchet cut him off.

"No, no," he said, "finish your dessert. This is very good cake, here. Ellie, you'll keep Clint occupied?"

"Yes, dear," she said. "When will you be back?"

"I don't know," Bouchet said. "This may keep me well into the night." He looked at Clint. "Again, I'm sorry. I'll make it up to you by taking you to my club."

"I'll look forward to it."

Bouchet nodded to Clint, kissed his wife on the cheek and left.

"You sonofabitch," Ellie said to Clint.

"Excuse me?"

"Which one did you fuck?"

"What are you talking about?"

"You know what I'm talking about," she said. "You couldn't have gone to the Lafitte house without sleeping with one of them. They're both tarts."

"They're both very nice ladies," Clint said. "And your husband was right, this is very good cake. What is this? Blueberry?"

"Yes."

"Delicious."

"Here," she said, pushing hers over. "Have mine. I've lost my appetite."

"What's wrong, Ellie?"

She crossed her arms and stared at him.

"Okay, I'll tell you," she said. "I haven't been able to stop thinking about you since last night."

"Ellie—"

"I'm not used to that," she said. "I've been with men before . . . like that . . . you know, once . . . and forgotten them the next moment. But not you."

"Well, I'm flattered," he said, "but you do have a husband."

"Oh, he knows what I do," she said.

"What? Does he know—"

"About us?" she said. "No, he doesn't know who I do it with, only that I do it. See, he . . . can't."

"Oh."

"So he's very understanding."

"I see."

"When I knew you were going to have lunch with . . . them, I knew one of them would seduce you."

"No one seduced me," he said, "except you."

"Oh, that's sweet," she said. "Can you assure me it'll stay that way?"

"Well, no," he said. "After all, I'm just a man."

"And they're tarts!"

"Ellie—"

"Yes, yes, I know," she said. "Finish that piece of cake and we'll go upstairs."

"Upstairs?"

"Well, you heard Francois," she said. "I'm to keep you occupied. Do you know of a better way?"

***

He followed her up the stairs and she took him to the same room.

"Who was that man who gave your husband that note?" he asked, while they undressed.

"That was Emile, my husband's secretary. Well, his right hand, actually."

"So Frankie left on business."

"Oh yes," she said. "He wouldn't have left otherwise."

She pulled the sheets down and got into bed. He set his gun on the night table.

"Does that really have to be there?" she asked.

"Yes." He turned and looked at the door. "Can we close it, this time?"

"Why?"

"If your husband comes back," he said, "I at least want enough time to jump out a window."

She laughed and said, "Go ahead, close it. And then get into this bed!"

Chapter Twenty-Two

Clint noticed that, as he got older, he was beginning to bend his own rules. A long-standing one was not to sleep with married women, but lately that one seemed to have fallen by the wayside.

Of course, a woman like Ellie Bouchet—beautiful, and without inhibitions—was difficult to resist. And, after all, he didn't know she was married, that first time.

She took pleasure from every appendage Clint had—fingers, tongue, mouth, cock—and let him have pleasure from every orifice she had—mouth, pussy, anus. They did it all, and eventually Clint even forgot to listen for Francois Bouchet's return.

Of course, she had told him her husband knew what she did, but if he didn't know who with, Clint was eager to keep it that way. He did not want to find himself challenged to any duels while in New Orleans.

Ellie finished him by riding his cock with abandon until, he finally exploded inside of her, causing her to collapse atop him, exhausted . . .

***

"Omigod!" she said, as they dressed.

"Yes," he said, breathlessly. "You don't think your husband came home while we were up here, do you?"

"No."

"How can you be so sure?"

"He doesn't come home quietly," she said. "He announces his presence as soon as he walks through the door."

They finished dressing, she took some time in front of the mirror, and then they went back downstairs. They were in the drawing room, with a drink each, when Francois Bouchet proved her point.

"I'm back!" they heard him shout, as he entered.

"In here, dear!" she called.

He entered and said, "Ah, yes, a drink. Good idea."

He poured himself a brandy.

"How did everything go?" she asked.

"Splendid," Bouchet said. "I managed to straighten things out more quickly than I thought I would." He looked at Clint.

"Business, you know."

"What kind of business are you in, Frankie . . . exactly?" Clint asked.

"Shipping, mostly," Bouchet said. "Import and export."

Bouchet finished his brandy and put the glass down.

"I think I am going to turn in," he said. "Clint, another night? When I can give you my full attention?"

Again, Clint looked for something—anything—insincere in the man's face, or his tone, but there was nothing.

"Eloise, you'll see Clint out?"

"Yes, darling, of course."

He walked to her, kissed her cheek and said to both of them, "Good-night."

They listened to him walk up the stairs.

"You say he knows what you do?" Clint asked.

"Yes."

"Then does he come in like that every time, to warn you?" Clint asked.

She thought about it, then laughed behind her hand.

"That never occurred to me," she said. "But no, I don't think he thinks that you and I . . ."

"I hope not," Clint said. "I like him."

"So do I," she said.

"I wouldn't want to do anything to hurt his feelings."

"Neither would I."

"Good," he said. "We're on the same page. Before I go, tell me something."

"What?"

"How many ships does your husband have for his business?"

"I don't know," she said. "I don't pay much attention to his businesses."

"More than one?"

"Yes," she said, "shipping is his main business, but he dabbles in others."

"What others?"

"Like I said," she replied, "I don't pay attention."

Clint finished his whiskey and put his glass down.

"I think I'd better go," he said. "I could use some sleep, as well."

"I'll walk you to the door."

As she did, he remembered Nina, the black maid, walking him to the door of the Lafitte house.

"Do you know Marguerite Lafitte's maid?"

"Nina. Yes, I do."

"Why do you know a maid?" he asked.

"Didn't Marguerite tell you?" Ellie asked. "Nina is supposed to be related to Marie Laveau."

"What? How? Daughter?"

"No, nothing that close," she said. "Second or third cousin, I think? Why?"

"As she was showing me out," Clint said, "she told me to be careful, that both Marguerite and Angelique are dangerous women."

"She's right," Ellie said. "They are."

Chapter Twenty-Three

The next afternoon Clint was in Pirate's Alley, alongside the St. Louis Cathedral, waiting for Angelique to appear. He had entered the alley from Jackson Square, but when she appeared, she was walking in from the opposite direction. She cut a dashing figure in trousers, a bright red blouse and thigh high boots.

"You're here," she said.

"I said I would be."

"I wasn't sure," she said. "I thought maybe we . . . scared you off."

"Not a chance," Clint said.

"Then you're not like most men."

"You mean the ones who have been proposing to you?" he asked.

"They either propose, or they run away," she said. "You haven't run away."

He smiled.

"I'm not about to propose, either," he assured her.

It was her turn to smile.

"Good," she said, "I would hate to start our association by turning you down. Shall we?"

"Where are we going?" he asked.

"To lunch."

"Where?"

"Right there." She pointed to a small café on one side of the square.

"And after lunch?" he asked.

"Let's get through lunch first," she said. "We have a lot to talk about."

"Lead the way, then," he said.

As they entered the café, a small man hurried over and gushed over Angelique.

"Miss Lafitte, it's a pleasure to have you here again."

"Thank you," she said. "This is my friend, Clint Adams. We'd like a table for two, somewhere quiet."

"Of course," he said. "Right this way."

He took them to a table away from all the others, in a corner.

"Will this do?"

"It's just fine," Clint said.

The man held Angelique's chair while she sat.

"I'll send your waiter right over," he said.

"Thank you." She looked at Clint. "When he gets here do you mind if I order for both of us? It will just be quicker."

"Please do."

When the waiter came she said, "Jambalaya for both of us."

"Yes, Ma'am."

"And champagne."

"Of course, Ma'am."

"Champagne?" Clint said. "Are we still celebrating something?"

"That remains to be seen."

"You look very dashing today," he said. "Like you should be standing on the deck of a pirate ship."

She smiled broadly.

"Thank you," she said. "That's just what I was going for."

"When do you intend to go looking for your grandfather's island?"

"As soon as I can put my hands on a ship."

"And how do you plan to do that?"

"Simple," she said. "I'm going to buy one."

"Do you have the money for that?"

"I do," she said. "I just have to find someone who wants to sell one."

The waiter came with the champagne, chilling in a bucket, opened it and poured it for them.

"Thank you," she said. As he left, she raised her glass. "To us."

"To us," Clint repeated, and they clinked glasses.

***

Francois Bouchet had an office in a building outside the French Quarter, that he used only for meetings with clients, or colleagues. Today he was meeting someone who came under another heading.

When there was a knock at his door, he opened it and said, "Come in. Have a seat."

Marguerite Lafitte entered and sat down across from him, as he seated himself behind the desk.

"What's happening?" he asked.

"Angelique is meeting with Clint Adams as we speak," she told him.

"That's good."

"Yes, it is."

"Why does he think they're meeting?" Bouchet asked.

"Something to do with Barataria Bay."

"Ah."

"Why am I here, Francois?" she asked.

"I thought we needed to talk," he replied, "somewhere we wouldn't be seen."

"Are you trying to protect your reputation, or mine?" she asked.

He shrugged.

"Maybe both."

"All right, then," she said. "Let's talk."

Chapter Twenty-Four

"Where do you expect to buy a boat?" Clint asked.

"Where else?" she replied. "On the docks."

"Do they know you down there?"

"They know my family."

"Your grandfather, you mean."

"Yes."

"And you think that will keep you safe down there?" he asked.

"No," she said, "I think you'll keep me safe."

"So you want me to go with you?"

"Yes."

"When?"

"Right after lunch," she said. "Do you have the time?"

"I have all the time in the world," he said. "I'm all yours."

"We'll talk about that another time," she said.

"And where's your mother going to be during all this?" Clint asked.

"She has her own business to see to," Angelique said.

"But she's behind you on this?"

"Let's just say she's not trying to stop me," Angelique replied.

The Jambalaya came and they got down to the business of eating it.

***

As they left the restaurant, Angelique took Clint's left arm.

"Let's get a cab to the docks," she said. "I don't feel like walking."

"No problem."

Jackson Square was a busy area, so waving down a cab proved to be no problem. They got an open-air carriage with one horse pulling it.

"The docks," Angelique told the driver.

"Yes, Ma'am." He was a young man, and his eyes widened as she got into his cab. Driving them, he kept glancing back at her.

When they reached the docks and got out, Clint paid the young man.

"Do you want me to stay and wait?" the driver asked Angelique. "It wouldn't be any trouble."

"That's all right," she said. "We'll be fine, but thank you for the offer. You're very sweet."

He blushed and almost fell from his seat, then turned and flicked the reins at his horse to pull away.

"Another conquest," Clint said.

"Jealous?" she asked.

"Not enough to challenge him to a duel," he said.

"Touché."

There was an eclectic collection of boats docked in front of them, but none seemed a likely pirate vessel.

"I don't see anything here that you could use," he said.

"You wouldn't," she said. "Not right out in the open, anyway. But somebody might have one for sale. We'll just have to ask."

"Well," he said, "you ask, and I'll stand by in case of trouble."

"Oh, there'll be trouble," she said.

"How do you know?"

"It follows me," she said. "The men down here will be ready to fight over me in no time."

"I'd say you have a big opinion of yourself," he said. "but you're probably right."

"If they want to fight each other, we won't have a problem," she said. "It's only if they want to fight you."

"Well, I don't think some dock worker is going to pull out a glove and challenge me, do you?"

"Not likely."

There were plenty of workers down by the water, and as they approached, she got all the attention she knew she would get.

"Come on down here," one man called. "I'll show you what a real boat is like."

"Not him," she said to Clint. "He's purely a worker, wouldn't have anything to sell."

"Then we should be up there," Clint said, "not down here." He pointed to some buildings that probably housed men who were more on the business end of what went on there.

"Good point," she said. "Let's go."

"Come on, darlin'," another man shouted. "Don't be like that."

"Want me to shoot him?" Clint asked.

"Just keep walking."

They reached a two story building where they could see men through the windows, sitting at desks or standing at file cabinets.

"There you go," Clint said. "Men in offices, rather than men on the docks. If nothing else, they should have better manners."

"We'll see," she said. "I find men are men, no matter where they are: docks, offices, or high society."

"Let's go find out," he suggested.

Chapter Twenty-Five

Clint and Angelique entered the building, found the stairs and ascended to the second floor, where the offices were.

A man came stumbling from one of the offices, like he wanted to be the first one to speak to Angelique.

"Can I help you?" he asked.

"Yes," she said. "I'm interested in buying a boat."

"Really?" The man was in his fifties and seemed surprised that a woman would want to buy a boat. "What kind of ship did you have in mind? Will you be hauling cargo?"

"A barque," she said, "preferably a three-master."

He seemed surprised that she knew exactly what she wanted.

"What's going on?" A man had come out of another office. This one was in his sixties, wore wire-framed glasses down on the end of his nose. He regarded Angelique above the glasses.

"This young lady was asking about a boat, Mr. Styles," the first man said.

"What about it, Stan?"

"Well, buying one," Stan said. "She wants a three-masted barque."

"What?" Styles said. "A pirate ship?" He looked at her again, then suddenly seemed to recognize her. "Come into my office, Miss." He looked at the other man. "Go back to work, Stan."

"Yes, sir."

"Thank you," she said.

She and Clint followed him. When they got inside, he walked around behind his desk.

"Have a seat," he said. "You're Angelique Laffite, aren't you?"

"That's right."

"And you?" he said to Clint.

"My name's Clint Adams."

"A pleasure, Mr. Adams," Styles said. "My name is Paul Styles." He looked at Angelique. "Miss Laffite, why would you be wanting a three-masted schooner?"

"A barque," she corrected.

"What's the difference?" Clint asked.

"A schooner has two or more sails," she said, "A barque has three or more."

"That's the basic difference, yes," Styles said.

"Were you testing me, Mr. Styles?"

"I might have been," the man admitted. "Tell me, what would you be using this ship for?"

"The same thing my grandfather used it for," she said, frankly.

Styles looked surprised.

"You want to be a pirate?" he said, laughing.

"Exactly."

Styles sat back in his chair and stared at her.

"You're kidding."

"I'm not," she said. "Do you have a ship I can buy, or not?"

Styles looked at Clint.

"What's your part in this?" he asked.

"I'm just here to back her up," he said, "in case of trouble."

"Trouble?" he asked. "What kind of trouble?"

"You know who she is, right?" Clint asked.

"I know who she is, who her mother is," Styles answered. "Heck, I even know who you are. What I don't know is why the Gunsmith would be needed in this situation. Unless you're looking to add pirate to your reputation?"

"Who knows?" Clint asked. "Right now, I'm just along for the ride."

Styles looked at Angelique.

"Can you afford to buy a barque?" he asked.

"I wouldn't be here if I couldn't," she said.

"And your mother?"

"What about her?"

"Is she involved in this?" Styles asked.

"Just me," Angelique said. "Mother has her own things going on."

Styles seemed to be considering the situation.

"Mr. Styles, if you can't help me, let me know, and I'll go elsewhere."

"Like where?" he asked.

"I didn't know you before I came here," she said. "I'm sure there are other men who can help me. I'll just have to find them."

"How about Francois Bouchet?" Clint asked.

"What?" Styles snapped. "What did you say?"

"Francois Bouchet," Clint said, looking at Styles. "He's involved in shipping." He turned his head and looked at Angelique. "I could ask him for you." He looked at Styles again. "We're friends."

"Miss Laffite," Styles said, "let me see what I can find for you. If you give me your address, I'll contact you when I have something."

"That'll be fine," she said.

He pushed a slip of paper over to her. She leaned forward and wrote her address on it, then stood up.

"Thank you, Mr. Styles," she said. "Good day."

"Good day to you, Miss," he said.

She and Clint left the office.

Chapter Twenty-Six

"Can you do me a favor?" Angelique asked when they got outside.

"Another one?"

"I think you know I'll make it worth your while."

"Go ahead."

"Would you ask Francois Bouchet about this man, Styles?"

"I can do that," Clint said. "And what if he says he has a ship he can sell you."

"I'll take it," Angelique said, "since you and he are such good friends—or are you better friends with Eloise?"

"You sure you want that favor?"

"I'm sorry," she said, raising her hands, "I didn't mean to pry."

"So what's your next step?" he asked.

"I'm actually supposed to be meeting a man in a saloon on Canal Street in about an hour."

"And do you need me for that?"

"Oh yes," she said, "I don't want him to think I need him for anything other than finding me a crew."

"Have you ever met this man before?"

"No," Angelique said, "the meeting was arranged for me."

"Canal Street," Clint said. "Do you want to take a cab again?"

She linked her arm into his left and said, "I think we can walk."

***

The saloon was rundown, with dirty windows that were virtually opaque, which Clint thought might have been deliberate.

"Oh yeah," he said, "you wouldn't want to go into this place alone."

"I might," she corrected him, "at some other time, if I was looking for something else."

"I'm sure you could handle yourself," he told her. "It's the men inside I'm worried about. I don't think they know the meaning of the word duel. You might just start a good old fashioned bar fight."

"I suppose we'll have to go inside and see, won't we?" she asked, with a smile.

"You're going to enjoy this, aren't you?"

"I'm going to enjoy our whole time together, Clint Adams," she said.

They entered the saloon, and immediately heads turned their way. Clint asked Angelique a question he should have asked her outside.

"What's this man's name?"

"Boyd."

"Is that a first or last name?" Clint asked.

"That's all I know," she said, "Boyd. Shall we go to the bar?"

"No," Clint said, "we'll go to a table and then I'll go to the bar and get us some drinks."

"Aw," she said, "you're trying to protect me."

"I told you," he said, "it's not you I'm trying to protect."

They walked to a back table and along the way Angelique smiled at some of the men they passed, who instantly sat up straighter.

"All right," Clint said, "you sit here and keep out of trouble, I'll be right back."

"I'll have a glass of wine," she said. "White, if possible."

"I'll see if this place has it."

Clint walked to the bar and noticed that nobody watched him. They were all still looking at Angelique.

"Do you have any white wine?" Clint asked the bartender.

"Sure, Mister," the man said, "but you're askin' for trouble bringin' a woman like that in here."

"It's not my idea," Clint said. "We're supposed to be meeting with a man named Boyd. He picked the place."

"Well, that figures."

"What's that mean?"

"Nothin'," the bartender said. "Boyd ain't here, yet. You want two white wines?"

"No," Clint said, "one white wine and a beer."

"Comin' up."

The bartender poured the drinks and set them down in front of Clint.

"What do I owe you?" Clint asked.

"Nothin'," the man said. "Just don't wreck the place."

"Why would we wreck the place?"

"You'll see," the man said. "When Boyd gets here, I'll send 'im over."

"Thanks."

Clint walked back to the table, wondering what that was all about, but then forgot it when he saw two men standing over Angelique.

"I'm sorry," he heard her say, "but I'm with someone."

"Yeah," one of them said, "but you could be with us."

"Let me put it this way," she said, with a smile, "not in a million years."

"Then why'd you come in here, bitch?" one asked, nastily.

"That's no way to treat a lady," Clint said, coming up behind them.

Both men—tall and broad-shouldered—looked like dock workers.

Clint put Angelique's white wine down in front of her, then turned to face the two men.

"I think the lady has made her feelings clear," he said. "Go away now."

"Go away?" one asked. He looked at his friend. "Go away, he says."

"I say it, too," another voice said, in a deep baritone.

Both men turned and looked at another man. He was big, beefy, and towered over them.

"Boyd!" one of them said. "Um, are they friends of yours?"

"They are," the big, black-bearded man said.

"We, uh, didn't know," the other man said. He looked at Angelique. "We're sorry, Miss."

The two men moved away.

"That beer for me?" Boyd asked, pointing to the one in Clint's hand.

"It is now," Clint said, and handed it to him.

Chapter Twenty-Seven

Clint got another beer from the bar, returned to find Boyd sitting across from Angelique. He pulled a chair over from another table and sat.

"This is Clint Adams," Angelique said.

Boyd looked surprised.

"The Gunsmith? Whataya doin' in New Orleans? This ain't the Wild West."

"I'm trying to get a little culture," Clint said.

Boyd laughed, and it boomed across the room.

"That's funny"! he said. "Culture, here?"

"You picked the place, Mr. Boyd," Angelique said, "not us."

Boyd stopped laughing and cleared his throat, trying to look serious.

"Yes, yes, of course I did, sorry, Miss," he said. "I understand you have some business to discuss with me."

"I'm in need of a crew," she said. "I've been told you're the man to see."

"Me?" he asked. "Somebody's kiddin' you. The only kind of crew I could put together would be a pirate crew," He laughed again.

"That's exactly what I want," she said.

He stopped laughing, stared at her, then looked at Clint.

"Is she serious?"

"Dead serious," Clint said.

Boyd looked at her again.

"You said your name is Angelique?"

"That's right," she said. "Angelique Laffite."

"Laff—" Boyd choked, drank some beer to clear his throat. This time he lowered his voice and said, with reverence, "Did you say Laffite?"

"That's right."

"Like Jean Laffite?"

She smiled.

"My grandfather."

Boyd sat back in his chair."

"So your mother is . . ."

". . . Marguerite Laffite."

"I hearda her," he said, folding his arms. "And I think I hearda you, too."

"What have you heard?" she asked.

"That you're trouble," Boyd said. "No wonder I hadda step in when I got here. You *are* trouble, aint'tcha?"

"I have been on occasion, yes."

Now Boyd leaned forward and asked with interest.

"Whatta you gonna do with a crew?"

"I'm going to take a ship out," she said, "and find my grandfather's Barataria Bay warehouse."

"Omigod!" Boyd said. "Is it really out there?"

"It is."

"And when you find it?"

She smiled.

"I'm going to start filling it," she told him. "I'm going to need a crew of about twenty who won't mind taking orders from a woman."

Boyd was done acting shocked and surprised. Instead, he looked excited.

"You're gonna need a First Mate," he said.

"Do you know someone who could do the job?" she asked.

"You're lookin' at 'im right here," he said, with a big smile.

"You'd be willing to First Mate to a female Captain?" she asked.

"I'd be First Mate to a Captain Laffite," he said. "You can damn well bet on that."

"How long would it take you to put together a crew?" she asked.

"A full crew? Quartermaster, boatswain, cabin boy, gunner, master, powder monkey—"

"The whole crew," she said, cutting him off. "Everybody."

"Days," he said. "How long will it take you to find a ship?"

"I'm working on it now," she told him. "We'll be looking at one in the next day or two."

"A two master? Or three?"

"Three," she said. "A barque."

"Good choice!" he said. Then he looked at Clint but spoke to Angelique. "And what position is he gonna fill?"

Angelique looked at Clint also and smiled.

"I don't know," she said. "I might just make him my cabin boy."

"I'm coming along for the ride," Clint told him. "Once we find what you're looking for in Barataria Bay, I'll be done and on my way."

"By God!" Boyd said, banging his hand on the table. "I think you're gonna get this done, Missy."

"In that case," she said, "you should probably call me something other than Missy, don't you think?"

The big man sat up straight, saluted and said, "Aye, aye, Cap'n."

Chapter Twenty-Eight

As Clint and Angelique left the saloon, he asked, "How many female pirates have there been?"

"Quite a few," she said. "Ann Bonny and Mary Read sailed with Calico Jack. They had to dress as men to be accepted, but they did it. And Rachel Wall, she was the first American woman to become a pirate during the seventeen eighties."

"What happened to her?"

"She was hanged in seventeen eighty-nine."

"And what about the other two?"

"Bonny and Read were sentenced to death," she said, "but their executions were stayed because they were both pregnant. Mary died in prison. Nobody knows what happened to Ann Bonny. She was one of the most famous female pirates of all time."

When they reached the street, they began to walk back toward the French Quarter.

"What now?" he asked.

"I'm going to head home," she said. "I have some plans to make."

"Do you want me to get you a cab?" he asked.

"No," she said, "I'm going to take the streetcar."

"Is that safe?"

She laughed.

"Very. Besides, I have this." She had a drawstring purse he hadn't paid much attention to. Now she opened it and showed him a two shot derringer.

"Not exactly a pirate weapon," he commented.

"A blunderbuss wouldn't fit in this purse," she answered. "What about you? What are you going to do?"

"I'll stop in and see Bouchet, see what he knows about the kind of ship you want."

"Will you be seeing Ellie?"

"I don't know," he said. "Frankie said he wants to take me to his club."

"Frankie," she repeated. "You and he *are* friends if he's got you calling him that."

"I suppose."

"Just be careful of Ellie," she said. "She's a dangerous woman."

"Dangerous in what way?" he asked.

"Just don't be alone with her," she said, "or you'll find out." She stood on her toes and kissed his cheek. "Thanks for your help."

"Wait," he said, "how will I contact you?"

"I'll send a message to your hotel," she said. "Don't worry."

He watched her walk toward the streetcar stop, then turned and headed back to his hotel.

When he got there, he found a message from Francois Bouchet. It said: "When you read this, come to my club," and it had a Bourbon Street address.

"When did this arrive?" he asked the clerk.

"Just about an hour ago, sir," the clerk said. "Is there a problem?"

"No," Clint said, "no problem. Thank you."

He went back out to the front of the hotel, where a doorman got him a cab, which he took to the Bourbon Street address.

***

As he disembarked from the cab, he could hear music coming from the open doors of several locations on the street. The building in front of him had a sign on the front that read THE STRATFORD CLUB.

There was a man barring the front door, but when Clint gave his name the man smiled, opened the door and said, "Go right in, sir."

Inside, a black man in a suit and white gloves greeted him and said, "Monsieur Bouchet is waitin', suh. This way, please."

Clint followed.

Chapter Twenty-Nine

Clint had been inside cattleman's clubs before, but he knew this was considered a "gentlemen's" club. Everything was leather and crystal as they walked the halls, and then entered a room filled with comfortable, expensive looking leather armchairs, with comfortable, expensive looking men seated in them. He spotted Bouchet even before the black man walked him over to him.

"Ah, my guest," Bouchet said, standing. "Thank you, Howard."

"Yes, sir."

"Howard?"

"His real name's Fabien, but Howard works better in this environment. Have a seat, Clint. Drink? Brandy?"

"Can I get a beer?"

"Of course." Bouchet waved a waiter over. "A beer for my guest, Edward."

"Yes, suh," the young black waiter said. Clint didn't bother to ask what his real name was.

"So what was on your agenda today?" Bouchet asked.

"I don't know if you'd call it an agenda," Clint said. "I spent the afternoon with Angelique Laffite."

"Ah," Bouchet said, "an erotic afternoon, I hope?"

"Not quite," Clint said. "She was looking for a ship and a crew. I just went along to keep her safe."

"Safe?"

"Well, she started on the docks and ended up in a Canal Street saloon."

"Ah," Bouchet said. "What kind of ship and crew was she looking for, and for what purpose?"

"Well," Clint said, "according to her . . . piracy."

Bouchet laughed aloud.

"Was she serious?" he asked.

"She seemed to be."

"But surely she's after something else," Bouchet said.

"I only know what she's told me, so far," Clint said. "And she wanted me to ask you something."

"Oh? And what was that?"

"Well, since one of your businesses is shipping, she wondered if you might know of someone selling a ship. A barque, she called it?"

"A three-masted schooner," Bouchet said. "Perfect for piracy—but, come on, you can't really believe that's what she wants it for."

"Considering who her grandfather was—"

"Who she claims her grandfather was," Bouchet said, cutting in. "It's never been proven."

"You don't think Marguerite knows who her father was?" Clint asked.

"I know who she says he was," Bouchet said, "but Marguerite is a woman who—how shall I put this . . . lies?"

"You've caught her in lies before?"

"Oh, many times," he said, "and not just me. You can talk to my wife about it."

"Maybe I will," Clint said. "If I'm going to continue to help Angelique, I'll have to satisfy myself she's being truthful."

"Piracy," Bouchet said, shaking his head. "Ah, here's your beer."

Clint accepted the glass from the waiter and said thank you.

"Well," Bouchet said, raising his brandy glass, "here's to Jean Laffite, the greatest pirate of all."

"Greater than Blackbeard?"

"Blackbeard didn't fight alongside Andrew Jackson, did he?" Bouchet asked.

"I suppose not."

"Are you free for supper tonight?" Bouchet asked. "I'll try not to get called away, this time."

"Sounds good."

"And you'll be able to talk to Ellie about the Laffite ladies."

"That sounds like a good idea."

"And maybe by then I'll know something about a barque," Bouchet offered.

"I'm sure Angelique will appreciate the effort," Clint said.

Bouchet stood up.

"I'm afraid I've got a meeting," he said, "but you can relax here and finish your beer. You have the run of the club as long as you're in New Orleans."

"I appreciate that," Clint said. "It's a very beautiful place."

"Yes, it is," Bouchet said, "it's the finest gentlemen's club in the French Quarter. Excuse me. See you tonight, around six?"

"I'll be there."

Bouchet nodded and left. Clint remained in the extremely comfortable leather chair and finished his beer.

Chapter Thirty

When Clint left the club, he thought he'd go back to his hotel and then to the Bouchet home for supper from there. When he arrived, he saw somebody waiting for him in the lobby, and was surprised.

"Nina!" he said. "What are you doing here?"

She rose from her seat and said, "Waitin' for you."

"Well," he said, "obviously, but why?"

"Can we go to your room to talk?" she asked.

"If you don't mind being seen going upstairs with me."

"I do not have a reputation I must worry about, Mr. Adams," she said.

She was wearing a simple green dress with a shawl around her shoulders. She pulled it tighter as she spoke.

"All right," he said. "Let's go."

They went up the stairs and to his room, which he unlocked and allowed her to enter.

"Would you like me to leave the door open?" he asked.

"Dat would be silly," she said.

"Fine." He closed it.

There was one chair in the room, in the corner. He grabbed it and dragged it to the center of the room.

"Have a seat, please."

She sat and he seated himself on the bed.

"Well," he said, "to what do I owe this pleasure?"

"It may not be a pleasure," she said. "You spent the mornin' and the afternoon wit' Miss Angelique."

"I did."

"What was ya doin'?"

"You don't know?"

"Dos ladies don't talk in front of me when they don't got to," Nina said.

"And why does it interest you?"

"I tol' you," she said. "Dos ladies are dangerous, Mister."

"Just call me Clint."

"Dey are dangerous, Mr. Clint," she said.

"In what way?"

"The t'ings dey do," Nina said. "Dey are not . . . safe."

"What things?"

"That's what I'm tryin' to find out from you!" she exclaimed, frustrated.

"Your accent is slipping, Nina."

The woman stared at him, then said, "Oh well, fine. So I don't have an accent."

"Then why the act?" he asked.

"It's the only way I could get hired to work in the Laffite house," she said. "People tend to think that all black Creole women are related to Marie Laveau."

"But you're not," Clint said.

"No, I'm not."

"Who are you related to, then?"

"No one of any importance," she said.

"And who are you working for?" he asked. "The Pinkertons? Are they worried about pirates, now?"

"Why would you think I'm a Pinkerton agent?"

"Because they like their subterfuge," Clint said. "They like going undercover."

"Well," she said, "I'm not a Pinkerton. I'm here on my own business."

"Which is?"

She didn't answer right away.

"Is your name even Nina?"

"No."

"What is it?"

Again, she didn't answer.

"Why do I get the feeling you want me to answer your questions, but you're not willing to answer mine?"

"I'd just like to know what you and Angelique did today, and then I'll leave you alone."

"I'm afraid it doesn't work that way," he said.

"What way does it work, then?" she asked.

"You give me something," Clint said, "and I'll give you something."

Nina bit her lip.

"You first," she said, then.

"I don't think so."

"Why not?"

"Because my experience with women here in New Orleans so far is that they're a bit . . . sneaky."

"That should be your experience wherever you go," she told him.

"Let's just deal with this trip, shall we?"

She bit her lip, then stood up.

"I'll have to think about it."

"That's fine," he said. "Let me know when you've made up your mind, and we can talk again."

She walked to the door.

"You won't tell them, will you?" she asked. "The Laffite women? That I'm not who I say I am."

"I think to do that I'd have to know who you actually are," he said, "and I don't know that yet. So, no, I won't be saying a word."

"Thank you."

"Yet!" he said, as she left.

Chapter Thirty-One

The Bouchets had a carriage pick Clint up at his hotel. Watching the scenery go by, Clint realized that, all-in-all, he hadn't seen much of New Orleans this trip. Just his hotel, the Bouchet house, the Laffite house, the docks and the gentlemen's club. As he knocked on the door of the Bouchet house, he decided to do some sightseeing in the morning, and maybe even some gambling in the evening.

The black house man opened the door for him and said, "This way, sir. Monsieur and Madame Bouchet are waitin' for you in the study."

This was the room with all the bookshelves where he had also met with Bouchet the night before.

"Clint," Ellie said, "how nice. Thank you, Zackary."

The black man left.

She was dressed casually, not in a dress you would expect a woman like her to greet company in. Maybe this was a good thing. They were considering him a friend. Likewise, Bouchet was wearing a smoking jacket rather than an expensive suit.

"I know you're not fond of brandy—" Bouchet started.

"Not if I have a choice."

"Whiskey, then?"

"Sure."

Bouchet poured a glass and handed it to him.

"Thanks."

"I better go and tell cook to get dinner on the table," Ellie said.

"No, no, dear," Bouchet said. "I'll do that. Clint has some questions for you."

"Oh? About what?"

"Not what," Bouchet said, on his way out of the room. "Who."

"Who's he talking about?" Ellie asked Clint.

"The Laffites."

"Ah, the pirate tarts!" She clapped her hands.

"Are you friends with Marguerite?" he asked.

"Of course."

"And Angelique?"

"No," she said, "Angelique is just my friend's daughter."

"As Marguerite's friend," he said, "do you believe that Jean Laffite was her father?"

"She says he was," Ellie said. "I don't have any reason to disbelieve her."

"But you say she's a tart."

"That doesn't make her a liar," she said. "As you know, I'm something of a tart, myself."

"Ah, so that's why you're friends," Clint said. "You have so much in common."

"Do we?" she asked, lowering her voice. "Has Marguerite taken you to bed, yet?"

"No."

"Don't be fooled by her age," Ellie said. "She's a very sexual woman."

"I can tell that by looking at her."

"Why are you asking if they lie?"

"Angelique says she wants to be a pirate like her grandfather."

"If that's what she says, I'd believe her," Ellie said. "It's crazy, but I'd believe her."

"Do you think her mother knows?"

"Oh yes," Ellie said, "those two are thick. They each know what the other's thinking."

"So you think Marguerite wants to be a pirate?"

"No," Ellie said, "that would be the young girl's dream."

"Supper!" Bouchet said, sticking his head in the room.

"We're coming, dear," Ellie said, slipping her arm through Clint's.

The table in the dining room was covered with food. They all sat, with Bouchet at the head of the table, Clint to his right and Ellie to his left.

"Dig in," Ellie said to Clint.

They all did, and this time no one came in to lure Bouchet away.

Afterward, Bouchet took Clint to the study again, this time for cigars and whiskey. Clint didn't usually smoke, but he never turned down a cigar.

"You said you and Angelique went to the docks today looking for a ship," Bouchet stated.

"That's right."

"Who'd you talk to?"

"A man named Styles."

"Paul Styles," Bouchet said, nodding.

"So you know him."

"Oh, yes. He's a thief. Tell your friend Angelique not to buy from him."

"Who should she buy from, then?"

"I will find her something," Bouchet said. "Something she can buy from an honest seller."

"It seems silly to worry about honesty," Clint said, "when she's talking about being a pirate."

"I see your point," Bouchet said, "but I still say she should stay away from Styles."

"I'll pass that on," Clint said. "Thanks for the supper, the whiskey, and the cigar, Frankie. Tell Ellie I said good-night."

"Sure, Clint," Bouchet said. "See you around."

"You can count on it."

"I'll walk you out."

Bouchet walked him to the door, promised to leave a message at his hotel if he found something for Angelique.

***

The same carriage took Clint back to his hotel, where thankfully nobody was waiting for him in the lobby.

"Any messages?" he asked the clerk.

"I'm sorry, sir, no."

"Thanks."

He went up to his room, took off his boots, sat on the bed and put his gun on the night table. His holster was hanging from the bed post.

Also on the night table was a copy of Edgar Allan Poe's *Tales of the Grotesque and Arabesque.* He opened it to "The Fall of the House of Usher," which he had already started, and read it to the end. The story explored themes of family isolation and madness.

Once he was done, and with no company, he laid down on the bed and got some sleep.

Chapter Thirty-Two

He woke up to a knocking on his door.

"Yeah. Okay!" he yelled. He grabbed his gun from his holster and carried it to the door. "Who is it?"

"The desk clerk, sir," a voice said. "I have a message for you."

Clint unlocked the door, opened it a crack, looked the clerk up and down, then opened it the rest of the way. The man took a couple of steps back when he saw the gun.

"Sorry." Clint held the gun behind his back, stuck out his left hand. "Message?"

"Yes, sir." The clerk handed it over. It was a white envelope, sealed.

"When did this come in?"

"About ten minutes ago."

"And who brought it?" Clint asked.

"I don't know." The clerk looked sheepish. "I left the desk for only a minute. When I came back it was there. I thought I'd better bring it up to you right away."

"Okay, thank you."

"Sir," the clerk said, and hurried off down the hall.

Clint closed the door, locked it, stuck his gun back in his holster, then sat on the bed with the envelope.

He took out a piece of white paper. A very flowery handwriting said: Meet me at the same Canal Street saloon tonight at ten. It was signed Angelique.

Had she heard from Boyd already about a crew? And why meet at that saloon so late?

He set the note aside and rubbed his face with both hands. There was no point in going back to sleep, since the sun was up. He washed up, put on a fresh shirt, and went out to get some breakfast.

***

The hotel was on Charles Street. He found a small cafe two blocks away that wasn't very busy, but that didn't matter. He had learned a long time ago that even the most rundown restaurants in the French Quarter had great food.

He went inside and was greeted by a spicy aroma. A waiter came over, drying his hands on an apron around his waist, and said, "Sit anywhere. No breakfast rush, yet."

"The back," Clint said.

"Suit yourself," the waiter said. "Coffee?"

"Please."

The waiter, a white-haired man in his sixties, came over and said, "Need a menu?"

"Is that andouille sausage I smell?" Clint asked.

"With Creole spices."

"And eggs?"

"In a casserole dish," the waiter said.

"That's what I'll have."

"Good choice. Biscuits?"

"Of course."

The waiter grinned.

"Comin' up," he promised.

He came back with the casserole dish and a basket of biscuits.

"Enjoy sir," he said.

"I intend to."

Clint found that he was ravenous and proceeded to wolf down the contents of the casserole dish. He was also aware that this was one of the rare meals he'd had while in New Orleans that he was actually paying for. So far the Bouchets and Laffites had been taking care of him.

People began to trickle in, some of them locals who looked over at him curiously. The waiter smiled and greeted many of them with familiarity, if not by name.

When Clint heard the waiter say, "'mornin', Boyd," he looked up, saw the big man he and Angelique had met in that Canal Street saloon.

"Table?" the waiter asked him.

Boyd pointed at Clint and said, "I'm joinin' him."

Chapter Thirty-Three

The big man walked over to Clint's table and sat across from him without invitation.

"Don't tell me you followed me here," Clint said.

"I did."

"Then you're light on your feet for a big man."

"These are my streets," Boyd told him.

"Well," Clint said, "that gives me an excuse for not seeing you. Breakfast?"

Boyd called the waiter over.

"I'll have what he's havin'."

"Okay, Boyd."

The waiter scurried off, came back with coffee for Boyd, then ran off to get the big man's breakfast.

"So what's on your mind?" Clint asked.

"That Laffite lady friend of yours," Boyd said. "Is she for real?"

"As far as I know."

"I mean, I've heard the rumors and all, but I never knowed if that was true."

"Then you know as much as I do," Clint said. "We either have to accept it, or not."

"I suppose so," Boyd said.

"Is that why you came to see me?" Clint asked.

"Pretty much," Boyd said, "except to tell you we're gonna have to be careful."

"Why's that?"

"There's fellas out there don't like them Laffite ladies," Boyd said.

"And what are they going to do?"

"I don't know," Boyd said, "but I'm doin' my best to keep them off the crew."

"And do we have a crew assembled?"

"Not yet."

"Then why does Angelique want me to meet her at that saloon tonight?" Clint asked. "Aren't we meeting you?"

Boyd shook his head.

"Not me," he said. "I ain't contacted her, yet."

"I don't like the sound of that."

Boyd sat back so the waiter could set his casserole down.

"You better get ahold of her and tell 'er not to go," the big man said.

"I'm going to do my best," Clint said, "but in case I can't find her, will you meet us there, anyway?"

"Sure thing," Boyd said. "We might as well find out what's goin' on, don't ya think?"

"I do," Clint said. "That's just what I think."

***

After breakfast, the two men left the little café together.

"You eat there a lot?" Clint asked.

"Not so much."

"The waiter knew you."

"Lots of people know me," Boyd said. "I kinda stand out."

"Yeah, you do."

"I'll be there," Boyd said, then started away.

"Not so fast," Clint said.

"What?"

"We got company, and I don't know if they're watching you or me."

Boyd looked around.

"You're good," he said.

"I didn't see you."

"Still . . . how do ya wanna play this?"

"We could split up, see who they follow. Then the other one can come up behind them."

"I like that," Boyd said.

"Okay, then," Clint said. "I'll head back to my hotel."

"I'll go the other way," Boyd said. "See ya."

As they split up Clint saw that he was the one being followed. He only hoped Boyd meant his parting remark.

***

They made their move before Clint could reach his hotel. They closed the distance on him, and he could see there were half a dozen of them. The gun he was carrying, the Colt New Line, had five shots in it.

"Hey, cowboy!" one of them yelled.

He stopped and turned.

"You talking to me?" he asked.

The six men were alike, young and brawny. Clint wondered if they were some of the men Boyd had been talking about, who didn't like the Laffites, or if they had been sent after him.

They all laughed.

"Who else would we be talkin' to?" asked the one who had been chosen as the spokesman. "You see any other cowboys on these streets?"

"Not at the moment."

"Well, there ya are," the man said. "We don't like cowboys in New Orleans."

The men all looked like dock workers, either bareheaded or wearing bandanas, with work shirts and jeans, and no guns. But they all had either a knife, or a club.

"I'm sorry to hear that," Clint said. "What do you plan to do about it?"

"Teach ya a lesson," the man said. "Just stand still. This'll only hurt for a minute. I promise."

Suddenly, there was nobody on his side of St. Charles Street. People saw what was going on and crossed over.

All but one.

Chapter Thirty-Four

"We know who you are," the man said. "We also know you can't shoot all of us."

"That's fine," Clint said. "Who wants to be first?"

"Right here on the street?" the man asked. "I don't think so."

"Maybe I don't even have to shoot," Clint said.

"Why not?"

"Because I'm not alone."

The man laughed.

"We saw you and Boyd split up outside the restaurant," he said.

"Then what's he doing behind you?" Clint asked.

"That's an old trick, Adams—" the man started, but when Boyd reached out and put a hand on the shoulders of two of the men and squeezed, they cried out in pain, cutting him off.

"Wha—" the front man said, turning to look. He was a tall, beefy man, but Boyd dwarfed him, as well as all the rest of them.

Clint stepped in and punched the man in the stomach. One of the other men came at him with a club, but Clint sidestepped and clipped him on the jaw.

Meanwhile, Boyd had driven two men to their knees, and now he reached out and smacked the last one in the face, knocking him out cold.

Both Clint and Boyd stepped up to the spokesman, who was bent over, trying to catch his breath.

"Who sent you?" Clint asked.

"Uh—uh—uh . . ." he gasped.

"Come on," Boyd said, "take a breath and tell us who sent you."

The man did take a breath, but it was a tortured one. They looked at the other five men, but none of them were in any shape to talk.

"Let's take him to my hotel," Clint suggested.

"Fine with me," Boyd said. He grabbed the man by the arm and said, "Let's go."

Boyd half dragged, half carried the man to Clint's hotel, where they then propped him up and walked him through the lobby between them. They only attracted attention because Boyd was so big.

When they got to the second floor Clint unlocked his door and Boyd threw the man into the room. He landed on the floor, tried to get to his knees. When he started to stand, Boyd slammed one hand down on his shoulder.

"Stay on your knees!" he commanded.

The man obeyed.

"What's your name?" Clint asked.

"They call me Knuckles."

"Why?" Clint asked.

"I hearda 'im," Boyd said. "He hands out beatin's with his hands." Boyd bent over so he could look the man in the eyes. "You wanna try me, Knuckles?"

"Boyd," Knuckles said, "this wasn't about you."

"Well, it is now," Boyd said, "so answer the man's question."

"Who sent you after me?" Clint demanded.

Knuckles hesitated, but when Boyd moved toward him he said, "Styles!"

"Why the hell would a businessman like Styles send you after me?"

"I don't know," Knuckles said. "He just told me to round up some men and to . . ."

"To what?"

". . . to make sure that when we wuz finished with you, you couldn't walk."

"So he didn't tell you to kill me?"

"No," Knuckles said. "He never sends me to do that. He says it'd attract too much attention."

"Well," Clint said, "now it's attracted my attention. Do you know anything about a meeting on Canal Street later tonight?"

"What? No, nothin'," Knuckles said. "We wuz just told to take care of you."

Clint looked at Boyd.

"I believe him," the big man said.

"Then I still need to find Angelique and warn her off," Clint said.

"Whatta ya wanna do with him?" Boyd asked.

"The others will go back to their boss and tell him what happened."

"No they won't," Knuckles said.

"Why not?" Clint asked.

"I work for Styles, but they work for me," he said. "They didn't know anythin' about Styles."

"Okay, then," Clint said to Boyd, "I want to send Mr. Styles a message."

"I'll—I'll take it to him," Knuckles promised.

"No," Clint said, "you won't."

"Why not?" Knuckles asked.

"Because, Knuckles," Clint said, "you're going to be the message."

Chapter Thirty-Five

Clint decided to go to the Laffite house in the Garden District, rather than try to send a message. He took a cab there, and when he knocked on the door, it was opened by Nina.

"Mr. Adams," she said.

"Is Angelique home, Nina?" he asked.

"No, sir, but Madam Marguerite is."

"I'd like to see her, then."

"Of course," Nina said. "Come in."

He entered and she closed the door, looked at him, and her face was saying things her voice couldn't.

"I'll tell Madam you're here," she said.

"Before you do that," he said, lowering his voice, "did you see Angelique go out?"

"Yes, this morning."

"Will she be coming back?"

"I don't know. You'll have to ask Marguerite. I'll go and get her."

"Thanks."

Nina walked across the entry foyer, her heels making clacking noises, on the floor. When she came back, she crooked her finger at him, rather than cross the floor again.

"She'll see you on the veranda," she said. Then she lowered her voice and added, "Watch yourself."

"Thanks for the warning."

"It's not a warning," she said. "It's advice."

"I'll remember."

He walked through the house to the veranda, found Marguerite sitting there, staring out at the garden.

"Where's Angelique?" he asked.

"Well, hello to you, too, handsome," she said, stretching languidly. She was wearing a silk robe that clung to her, outlined the nipples of her large breasts. "Have a seat. Drink?"

"No, thanks," Clint said. "Where's Angelique?"

"I don't know," Marguerite said. "She went out this morning. Why, what's wrong?"

"She's meeting a man at a saloon on Canal Street tonight."

"So?"

"The man she thinks she's meeting says he didn't send her a message."

"Oh, my. What's that mean?"

"It means she could be in trouble if I don't get to her first."

"And if you don't?"

"Then I'll be at that saloon tonight, too."

"Well then," she said. "You've got time."

"Time for what?"

She smiled, unbelted her robe and opened it. She was naked underneath. Her heavy breasts were tipped with pink nipples, her skin was smooth and pale, and the bushy hair between her legs was dark as night. Her body was certainly not a sixty-year old woman's body.

"Time for us to get better acquainted."

"While your daughter may be out there in trouble?" he asked.

"According to you," she said, coming up out of the chair she was sitting in, "she won't be in trouble until tonight." She put her hand on his crotch. "That gives us plenty of time, and then you have time to still find her."

"Marguerite—"

"Shh," she said, and silenced him with a kiss. She pressed her entire body against him, and he couldn't help but react. "Mmm, I see your body agrees with me," she said, rubbing him through his trousers.

"Marg—"

"You have to stop talking and give in," she whispered. "That's the only way this is going to get done."

She undid his trousers, and as they fell to his ankles, he set his gun down on the nearby table. She got down on her knees, tugged his underwear down and then reared back as his cock sprang forward, almost hitting her in the face.

"My, you could take a woman's eye out with that thing." She leaned forward and kissed the spongy head of his penis. "That is an impressive *zozo*."

"A what?"

"*Zozo*," she said. "That is the Creole word for your tallywacker."

She opened her mouth and took his zozo inside. She sucked it for a while, rubbing her hands up and down his thighs, and cupping his ass cheeks, until he was gritting his teeth to keep from exploding into her mouth.

She released him, bent over the table with her arms and hands supporting her, shook her ass at him and said, "Come, let's get acquainted."

He got behind her, slid his cock up between her thighs and into her soaking wet vagina, and began to fuck her hard. If this was what she wanted, he was going to give it to her good.

She grunted or moaned every time he drove into her. He felt every muscle in her body stiffen, and then go limp as waves of pleasure coursed through her. He pumped in and out, faster, seeking his own release, and when it came, he slammed his cock in tightly and bellowed out his own pleasure . . .

Chapter Thirty-Six

There was a cloth napkin on the table next to a tray with a decanter and some glasses on it. She cleaned herself before picking up her robe and putting it back on. Then she sat down.

"Now I need to catch my breath," she told him.

He had pulled up his underwear and trousers, wondering how he managed not to trip and tumble over with them around his ankles, since he still had his boots on the entire time. He secured his belt, then picked up the gun from the table and stuck it into his belt. Neither of them had even bothered to remove his shirt and jacket.

He poured himself a drink from the decanter and drained it in one swallow.

"Pour me one, will you, dear?" she asked.

He did and handed it to her, then poured another for himself. He sat down because his legs were weak and, yes, he also had to catch his breath.

"Marguerite," he said. "you must have some idea where Angelique went."

"*I* must have?" she asked. "You have more knowledge about what my dear daughter has been up to then I do."

"That's bull crap," he said. "You know exactly what she's planning."

"Oh, don't tell me it's that pirate thing, again?" she asked. "Yes, I know about that, and I've tried to talk her out of it."

"What else is she interested in?" he asked. "Where else could she have been goin'."

"To tell you the truth, darling, I thought she was going to your hotel for a repeat of your little tryst in the garden."

"The garden," he said.

"In the maze?" she said. "I watched from my window. Very entertaining. Now you've had mother and daughter, what do you think? How do I measure up?"

"Well, what can I say," Clint answered. "You're the original, right?"

"Exactly."

She sipped her drink, looking like she was breathing normally again. He was still trying to get there.

"Marguerite," he said, "I've got to find her."

"Oh, all right," she said. "Sometimes she just goes to Jackson Square to walk around, have lunch, look at the art, stare at the Cathedral, and think about her grandfather."

"Okay," he said, "I'll try that. If she comes home, tell her not to go to Canal Street tonight. And send me a message at my hotel. If I don't hear from you, I'll be there tonight."

"Then you'll keep her safe, no matter what," Marguerite said. "I needn't worry."

"You can worry a little," he said. He drained his second drink and set the glass down. It was brandy. He needed a beer.

On his way to the front door, he encountered Nina again. She gave him a disapproving look.

"Sometimes you just have to do what you have to do to get answers," he said.

She made a rude sound with her mouth.

***

After Clint left, Nina went back to the veranda, where Marguerite was still lounging in her chair.

"Nina, be a dear and pour me another drink, will you?" she asked.

"Yes, Ma'am."

Nina took the glass from Marguerite's hand, poured the drink, and handed it back.

"You heard?"

"Yes, Ma'am," Nina said. "it was hard not to."

"He lives up to his reputation," Marguerite said. "At least that side of it. I just hope he can live up to the other side, as well."

"Yes, Ma'am. I hope so, too."

She left Marguerite to her drink.

***

At Jackson Square Clint walked around, looked in the park at the center, walked around the St. Louis Cathedral, as well as inside, then strolled the park, keeping his eyes open for Angelique. But there was no sign of her. He wondered if Marguerite had even told him the truth?

After an hour he had a quick bite to eat in the same restaurant he and Angelique had eaten in before and asked the waiter if he had seen her.

"Not since you and she were here, sir."

"Okay, thanks."

He left, stopped just outside the restaurant for one last look around. He realized he had made a mistake. He should have gotten a location from Boyd, where he could get ahold of him. Now he was just going to have to wait until that night, on Canal Street, to see both Boyd and Angelique, hopefully before something bad happened.

Chapter Thirty-Seven

There were no messages at the hotel desk, so Clint went to his room to consider his next move. Unfortunately, there wasn't one. It wouldn't do any good to go looking for Angelique all over the French Quarter and the Garden District. He'd just have to go to Canal Street and wait.

And he'd have to get there early . . .

***

Angelique's note said to meet her there at ten. Instead, he walked into the place at eight-thirty. There was no room at the bar, and most of the tables seemed to be taken. As before, the customers looked like dock workers.

"So you're back," someone said.

He turned, saw the three men who had been bothering Angelique.

"And you don't have your big friend with you, this time," the man said. "Or your woman."

"I'm meeting both of them here," Clint said. "I'd advise you three not to be here."

"But we're here now," one of the others said.

"Look," Clint said, "we're all standing in front of the bar. How about I buy you boys a beer?"

The three men looked at each other, then the first one said. "Sounds good. Let's get a table."

***

Clint had meant to buy them a beer and then sit at a table alone, but instead he ended sitting with the three of them. He was going to try to get them to leave after one beer, but, in the end, he thought they would be good camouflage. He could go unnoticed until Boyd or Angelique walked in.

Boyd said he hadn't contacted Angelique to set up this meeting, but that he would come along, anyway.

While the three men drank, got drunk and talked among themselves, effectively forgetting he was even there until it came time for more beers, Clint kept scanning the interior. There were a few men who kept glancing at the front door, as if they were waiting for someone. Maybe one or more of them were waiting for Angelique.

Finally, about ten minutes to ten, Angelique walked in the front door. Naturally, she drew everyone's attention.

"There's your gal," one of the men said to Clint. "Want us to get 'er and bring 'er over here?"

The three of them started to get up, but before Clint could say anything, they all fell back into their chairs, too drunk to walk.

"I'll do it," Clint said.

He stood up and walked to where Angelique was standing, just inside the door.

"We have to leave," he said, taking her arm.

"But I just got here. I'm supposed to meet Boyd—"

"I saw Boyd today. He didn't send you that message."

"What? Then who—"

"Later," Clint said. "Let's get out of here now."

He almost pushed her out the door, but then stopped. There was no point in sending her out first.

"Stay behind me," he said.

She didn't argue. They walked out with Clint shielding her. The first bullet hit him in the arm, but after that he was moving, dragging her down and to the side as more lead came flying at them from across the street.

Angelique screamed as Clint pushed her to cover behind a horse drawn cab. The break was on, which kept the skittish horse from running off, but that wouldn't last.

"Stay here!" Clint snapped, taking out his gun.

He moved around behind the carriage, then ran across the street and sought cover in the shadows. He looked further down the street, saw the muzzle flash when somebody fired again, blindly. He fired into the flash and somebody cried out. After that he heard footfalls, as more than one man ran from the scene.

"Adams!" The voice came across the street.

He looked over at the saloon, saw Boyd standing in the light. He realized how spotlighted he had been when he came out of the saloon. Luckily, somebody was a bad shot.

He broke from his cover and ran back across the street to Angelique.

"Are you all right?" he asked, helping her up.

"Yes, I think so," she said. "Y-you saved my life."

"You two okay?" Boyd asked, coming over to join them. "I heard the shooting just as I turned the corner."

"The shooters are gone," Clint said. "There was more than one."

"How could you tell?" Boyd asked.

"I heard more than one gun," Clint said, "and then heard when they ran off. I'd say at least three."

"Why would they wanna kill you?" Boyd asked.

"It wasn't me they were after," Clint said.

"Clint's hurt!" Angelique said, noticing the blood on his left arm.

"Let's get back inside and take care of that," Boyd said.

Chapter Thirty-Eight

Inside the saloon, they got Clint to a back table, where Boyd tore the sleeve off his left arm. The bullet had taken a chunk from his arm and kept going. The bartender provided hot water and cloth for bandages. Angelique cleaned the wound and wrapped it tight while the other customers remained where they were and watched. The three men Clint had been drinking with had their heads down on their table.

"There," she said, "that's not too bad, but you should see a doctor."

"Tomorrow," Clint said. He looked at Boyd. "Why do you think they picked this place for an ambush?"

"I guess whoever it was knows that we met here before," Boyd said. "But you said they weren't after you."

"They sent Angelique a message, which was supposedly from you, to meet here at ten," Clint said. "If she hadn't sent me the same message, she'd be dead, right now."

"But . . . why?" Angelique asked. "What have I done?"

"I don't know," Clint said. "It could be all this pirate talk, but why? I'll find out tomorrow."

"How?"

"Styles sent some men after me, as well," Clint said. "I've got to assume he sent these, tonight."

"He'd rather kill me than sell me a ship?"

"That's what I'm going to find out." Clint looked at Boyd. "How are you doing assembling a crew?"

"I'm close," he said. "I need a quartermaster, and a gunner."

"Well, keep trying," Clint said. "We're not going to let this stop us." He looked at Angelique. "Unless you want to stop."

"Hell, no!" she said. "I want to do this more than ever. Somebody must know something about Barataria Bay. That's the only reason I can think of for them not to want me to go."

"You have a good point, there," he said. "Come on, I'll see you home."

"You want me to come, too?" Boyd asked.

"No," Clint said, "but do me a favor. Check the doorways directly across the street and see what you can find."

"What am I lookin' for?"

"Anything," Clint said. "Something to tell us how many there were, what they were shooting . . . I heard a rifle. Look for ejected shells."

"Okay," Boyd said. "I'll take care of it."

"Thanks."

"Wait here," Boyd said, "I'll go out and find you a carriage to take you back."

As Boyd left, the bartender came over with a whiskey and a beer. "You look like you could use this. On the house."

"Thanks," Clint said.

As the bartender walked away Angelique asked, "Do you want the whiskey or the beer?"

"I'll take the beer."

"Good." She grabbed the whiskey. "I need this." She tossed it down.

Clint drank half his beer, then looked around. They were still getting attention, but he knew it had nothing to do with him. It was Angelique's long dark hair and pale, beautiful face. The dress she wore covered her from neck to ankles, but in between it clung to her enough to show off her body.

"What were you doing today?" Clint asked. "I was looking for you all day so we could avoid this."

"I can't totally depend on Boyd for a crew," she said. "I was out talking to people."

"Did you find anybody?"

"No," she said. "And I talked to some old timers who claim they used to be pirates. They had nothing to say about Barataria Bay." She picked up his beer and took a sip. "Did you talk to Bouchet?" she asked.

"Yes," Clint said, "he had nothing good to say about Styles, and after today I agree with him."

"What are you going to do tomorrow?"

"I'm going to put it to Styles point blank," Clint said, "and find out why he'd rather get rid of us than have us outfit a boat."

"Ship," she said.

"Whatever."

Boyd came in and waved. They got up and joined him at the door.

"I got a driver and carriage to take ya where you wanna go," he said. "Cap'n, I'm real close to havin' a crew, but if you get another message that's supposed to be from me, it ain't unless it's signed "Horace.""

"Horace?" she said.

"Yeah," he said. "That's my first name, and I never use it."

"Well," she said, with a smile, "thank you for trusting me with it, Horace."

The big man winced and took them out to their carriage.

Chapter Thirty-Nine

Clint saw Angelique home, but didn't go in with her. He really didn't want to be in the same room with mother and daughter, at the moment.

"So you'll be going to see this man Styles tomorrow?" she asked.

"Yes."

"Shall I come with you?"

"No," he said, shaking his head, "I'm not expecting it to go smoothly."

"Will you let me know what happens?" she asked.

"Definitely."

"And will you go see a doctor about your arm?"

"Yes," he lied, since there was really no need.

"And what about Bouchet?"

"I'll see what he has to say about a boat."

"Ship."

"Yes, right," he said. "Good-night, Angelique. Get some sleep."

"You, too, Clint."

He watched after her until she went inside, then returned to the carriage and told the young driver to take him to his hotel.

"Wait!"

They both turned to see who had spoken. Nina was running toward them. She was holding a wrap tightly around her. "Can you give me a ride?"

"Where to?" the driver asked.

"Just take me wherever you're takin' him," she said, pointing at Clint.

"Get in," the driver said, liking what he saw.

Clint reached out and helped Nina into the carriage. She lost her balance and fell into his lap. Despite himself, his body reacted immediately not only to the feel of her long and lean body, but the smell. It was heady, and more than just perfume. It was her.

"I'm sorry," she said, shifting to the seat next to him.

"No problem," Clint said, as they pulled away from the house.

"Where are you off to?" Clint asked.

"I just wanted to get out of that house," she said.

"Did you see Angelique when she came in?"

"No," Nina said, "we missed each other."

"Do you like her?"

"No, but nobody does—except maybe you. But then, you like her mother to, don't you?"

Clint winced and said, "So you heard us?"

"How could I not?" she asked. "I have to say, it excited me." She put her warm hand on his leg. "I mean, I like my sex soft and quiet, but what you and she did . . . it was oddly exciting." She giggled, tightening her hand on him. "I almost came out and joined you."

"How would Marguerite have reacted to that?"

"I don't know," Nina said, "but how would you have reacted?"

She didn't wait for him to answer. She leaned over and kissed him, letting her tongue flutter in his mouth. He kissed her back, enjoying the taste of her. It was quite different from Angelique and Marguerite, very unique.

Her hand moved from his thigh to his crotch and squeezed him.

"I should've joined you," she said, "but let me show you how to be quiet."

She unbuttoned his trousers, reached in and grabbed his hard, hot cock.

"Nina," he started, but she waved him off with her other hand, held her finger to her full lips, and pointed at the back of the driver's head.

Then she pulled his hard cock out of his trousers, lowered her head and engulfed it with her mouth. She proceeded to suck him avidly, but quietly, and he bit his lips to keep from groaning out loud.

It seemed like the women of New Orleans like having sex where they might get caught. First Ellie in her own house, in a room with the door wide open, and now Nina in the back of a carriage, where the driver only had to look back.

Her head bobbed up and down faster and faster until, finally, he exploded into her mouth, and almost bit through his bottom lip trying to be quiet.

She sat up, wiped the corners of her mouth with her thumb and forefinger, and smiled at him.

"You see?" she said. "Quiet, but still exciting."

He adjusted himself and buttoned his trousers. The driver never looked back.

***

At the hotel Clint stepped down, reached up to help Nina.

"No," she said, "I have someplace else to go. Can the driver take me?"

Clint looked at the young man.

"Sure thing."

Clint gave him some money.

"Thank you, sir." As Clint went into the hotel on unsteady legs, he heard the man ask, "Where to, Ma'am."

He didn't hear the answer.

Chapter Forty

The next morning, after a quick breakfast, he went down to the docks to the office of Paul Styles. He entered the building, headed for the stairs he knew would take him to Styles' office, but before he could get there, he saw some men he recognized. It was three of the men who had attacked him on the street. And now they moved to block his path to the stairs.

"Hey," they said, "you come back to give us another chance?"

"No chances," Clint said, producing his Colt New Line. "Move out of the way."

"You ain't gonna shoot us," one man said. "Not here."

"And we ain't armed," another said.

"I don't care," Clint said. "I'll shoot first and then explain my reasoning later. I'm not about to let you three pound me into the ground."

"No guts," another said.

"Oh? How about we go one-on-one?" Clint asked. "Just me and one of you. I lose, I'll leave. I win, I get to go up those stairs. Whataya say?"

The three men studied him for a moment considering their options, but were saved from having to make a choice.

"I say step aside, let the man through," Paul Styles called from the top of the stairs, "before he shoots you all in the knees."

Reluctantly, the men parted and allowed him to walk to the stairs.

"I've been expecting you," Styles said.
"You mean after your men missed their chance the last time?"

Clint asked.

"I don't know what you mean, Mr. Adams," Styles said. "Come on up."

The men watched Clint as he went up the stairs. When he got to the top, Styles had already walked to his office door. He waited there for Clint to reach him.

"Come on in and have a seat," Styles said. "I may have somethin' for you and your lady friend."

"Angelique is the one you'd be dealing with," Clint said. "Not me."

"Of course, of course."

"But you have to deal with me on another matter."

"And that is?"

"Sending your men after me."

"I told you," Styles said, "I don't know anythin' about that."

"That's not what your man told me," Clint said.

"Obviously somebody's tryin' to implicate me," Styles said.

"Look, do you want to do business or not?"

"I'd say not, since reliable sources tell me you're something of a thief," Clint said. "I'm telling you to stay out of my way."

Styles stood quickly.

"This is my town, Adams, not yours," he said. "I think you're the one who better stay out of *my* way."

"I guess we'll see," Clint said.

He turned and stormed out of the office, stopped at the top of the stairs when he saw not only the three men who had attacked him in the street waiting at the bottom, but three more—six in all.

Styles came out of the office behind him, looked down and said to the six men, "Let him leave only if he can get past you."

The six men grinned and nodded. Three took out knives, the other three clubs.

Clint turned, pulled out his Colt New Line and shot Styles once in the shoulder. The man staggered, his eyes going wide with shock. Before he could fall, Clint was on him, holding him up.

"You're going down the stairs ahead of me," Clint said to him. "If I don't get out, neither will you, got it?"

"You—you shot me!"

"I'm glad you noticed."

"I'm—I'm bleedin'," Styles said. "I need a doctor."

"Sure," Clint said, "after you walk me out of here."

"Y-you're crazy!"

"Move!"

Clint settled his left hand on Styles' uninjured shoulder from behind, held his gun pressed to the small of the man's back.

"Nobody can survive a bullet here," he said, pressing harder. "Remember that."

They started down the stairs.

"Whatta we do, Mr. Styles?" one of the men asked.

"Get the hell out of the way!" Styles yelled. "And get me a doctor."

One of the men ran from the building to find a doctor. The others spread out to let Clint and Styles pass.

"If there's anybody waiting outside," Clint said, "you're dead."

"Y-you shot an unarmed man," Styles accused.

"You were armed," Clint said, "with six bully boys."

He walked Styles outside, followed by the remaining five men. There were no others waiting on the docks.

"Tell them to go back inside," Clint instructed him.

"Get back inside, all of you!" Styles yelled.

Blood was flowing down his arm and dripped from his fingers.

"Jesus," he said, "it hurts . . . I need a doctor."

"That's up to you and your men," Clint said.

"I'll have the law on you!" Styles snapped.

"You do and they won't be able to stop me from killing you."

"Y-you'll go to prison! Be hanged."

"You won't see it," Clint said, "because you'll be dead."

Clint walked the man to the end of the docks. Once he was sure nobody was following them, he released his hold on the man's shoulder. Immediately, Styles went down to his knees.

"A-am I gonna die right here?" he asked.

"I shot you in the shoulder, you weakling," Clint said. "Don't tell me this is the first time you've ever been shot."

"Of—of course it is!" Styles said.

"That's hard to believe," Clint said, "given your personality."

Clint stuck the New Line back into his belt and strode away from the docks.

Chapter Forty-One

Clint went from the docks to the Bouchet house. He wanted to talk to Francois. The door was answered by Zackary, the black house man.

"Zackary, is Mr. Bouchet here?"

"No, sir."

"Is he at his club?"

"Either there or his office, sir."

"I'm supposed to meet with him, but I forgot the address he gave me for his office."

"I can give you his card, suh," Zackary offered.

"Thank you."

Zackary went into the house, came back with the card and handed it to Clint.

"Uh, sir, Madame is home. Do you wish to see her?"

"No, Zackary, thank you. I'll just go and find Mr. Bouchet."

"Very well, sir," Zackary said. "Have a good day."

"You, too."

Clint left, hoping Zachary wouldn't tell Ellie he had been there.

***

Clint tried Bouchet's club first, and was told he wasn't there, so he then took a carriage ride to Bouchet's office, which was in a building outside the French Quarter. When he stepped down from the carriage, he could immediately see the difference between the Quarter and this, New Orleans' business district. He wondered if Paul Styles had an office here as well as on the docks?

He found the building and read the directory on the wall of the lobby. Bouchet's office was on the second floor of the four story structure. There was an elevator in the building, but Clint didn't like elevators, so he took the stairs.

On the second floor, he found the door that said BOUCHET INDUSTRIES and entered. Inside, he found himself being stared at by a very officious looking middle-aged woman, seated at a desk.

"Yes?" she asked. "What is it?"

"I'm here to see Mr. Bouchet," he said.

"Do you have an appointment?"

"No," he said, "but . . . Frankie said I could stop by any time."

He thought the use of Bouchet's nickname might soften her glare, but it didn't.

"And your name?"

"Clint Adams."

"Please wait here."

She stood and went through a door that apparently led to his office. When the door opened again, moments later, she stood aside and said, with great disapproval, "You can go in, sir."

"Thank you."

He entered the office and was welcomed expansively by Francois Bouchet.

"Clint! My friend! Welcome. A drink?"

"Not today, thanks, Frankie."

"What brings you here, my friend? Oh, is it the matter of a ship for Angelique, the lady buccaneer?"

"I shot Paul Styles," Clint said.

Bouchet looked shocked.

"What?"

Clint explained what had happened, what had led up to his shooting of Styles.

"Is he dead?"

"I doubt it," Clint said. "I shot him in the shoulder." The remark reminded him that his own wound ached, but it wasn't as bad as Styles'.

"While he was unarmed?"

"He was armed with six men he was sending after me," Clint explained.

"I see. I assume the police will be looking for you?"

"I don't know," Clint said. "Is Styles the kind of person who would go to the law? After all, he sent his men to hurt me, maybe kill me."

"No," Bouchet said, "he wouldn't call in the law. He would take care of things, himself."

"I told him if he comes after me again, I'll kill him."

"Well," Bouchet said, "he never does it himself. You say he sent six men after you?"

"Yes."

"He might send more," Bouchet said. "You're going to need to watch your back, Clint."

"I think I've got just the man who can help me with that, Frankie," Clint said. "But what about Angelique's ship?"

"Clint," Bouchet said, "is she really serious about this pirate thing?"

"She's getting a crew together," Clint said, "so I think the answer's yes."

"Well then," Bouchet said, "I think I've got a ship."

Chapter Forty-Two

Clint didn't know where to find Boyd. But he knew about the saloon on Canal Street, so he went there. It was open, and the bartender was behind the bar, but there were only two customers in the place.

"Hey," the bartender said to him, "you're Boyd's friend. Kinda early, ain'tcha?"

"I need to find Boyd," Clint said. "Do you know where he lives?"

The fortyish bartender frowned and said, "I thought you was friends."

"New friends," Clint said. "I just don't know where he lives."

"I-I can't tell ya that," the barman said. "He wouldn't like it."

"Could you send him a message for me?"

"Huh? Oh, sure, I can do that."

He got a piece of paper from the bartender and wrote a message to Boyd, saying he had to see him because he thought he was going to need backup. He asked Boyd to come to his hotel. He folded the paper and gave it to the bartender.

"When can you get this to him?"

"I'll have one of these fellas run it over there," the bartender said. "Boyd'll have it today."

"Thank you," Clint said. "I appreciate it."

As he was leaving, he heard the bartender yell, "Hey, Quinn! I got a job for ya."

***

He knew he could have followed Quinn to Boyd's house, but decided against it. He thought the big man would respond to his call for help. So he flagged down another carriage and took it to the Laffite house, in the Garden District. During the ride, he flexed his injured arm. He'd been shot enough times to know the wound wasn't serious, but the arm still ached, and was stiff.

Nina answered the door and smiled at him.

"You come for me, or them?" she asked him.

"I've got business with Angelique," he said. "That's all."

"Business?"

Clint nodded.

"Well, come in, then," Nina said. "I'll tell 'er you're here."

She left him just inside the door, then came back and said, "They're both on the veranda. You know the way."

"Thanks, Nina."

He made his way through the house to the veranda, where both women were seated, having tea and cakes.

"Come, join us," Marguerite invited him.

"Thanks."

He sat and relaxed, because he figured Styles could not exact any vengeance against him there.

"Did you see Styles?" Angelique asked.

"Yes."

"What happened?"

"I shot him."

"What?"

Both women sat up straight. He explained exactly what had happened.

"Is he going to come after you?" Marguerite asked.

"I don't know," Clint said. "At the time I didn't think he would, but now I'm not so sure. He just might send more men."

"You're going to need some help," Angelique said.

"I think I know where I can get it," Clint said.

"Bouchet?" she asked.

"Boyd," he said.

"Ah . . ."

"Why not Francois?" Marguerite asked.

"I'm using him for something else," he said, and then looked at Angelique. "He says he has a ship for you."

"Oh my God," Marguerite exclaimed to her daughter. "You have a ship?"

"And a crew," Clint added.

"I don't believe it!"

"Marguerite, did you think Angelique wasn't serious about this?"

"She's been talking about being a pirate since she was a little girl," Marguerite said. "I guess this proves she never got over it."

"So this is all a surprise to you?"

"Well," Marguerite said, "I wouldn't call it a surprise, but . . . I suppose she's going to try to live her life's dream."

"So what do you think she'll find when she gets to Barataria Bay?"

"First," Marguerite said, "she'll have to find Barataria Bay. Then she'll have to find the right island. Finally, when she finds the warehouse, who knows what—if anything—will be in it."

"So what do I do now?" Angelique asked him.

"You go and see Bouchet and make your deal," Clint said.

"And what are you going to do?"

"I've asked Boyd to meet me at my hotel," he said. "I think I can count on him for some backup, if I need it."

"For when Styles comes after you?" Angelique said.

"According to Bouchet," Clint said, "Styles would never come for me himself. He'll send men."

"What about the police?" Marguerite asked. "I mean, you did shoot him."

"Bouchet also said he doubts Styles would go to the law," Clint said. "After all, he's a thief."

"What about you?" Marguerite asked. "Why don't you go to the law?"

"I don't want to do that, either," Clint said. "I might end up in jail, myself."

"So this will all be handled between the two of you," Marguerite said.

"That would be preferable," Clint said.

"What about a duel?" Angelique asked.

"What?"

"Why don't you challenge Styles to a duel?" she said. "That way the two of you can settle it, and nobody will be the wiser."

"Except for the seconds," Clint said, "and whatever witnesses there might be."

"I'll be your second," Angelique said. "And you can make sure there are no witnesses."

"That leaves his second," Marguerite said, "and since you've already shot him, you would probably have to face his second."

"That's a good point," Angelique said. "And if that's the case, his second is liable to be a professional."

"A professional second?" Clint asked.

"A professional duelist," Marguerite corrected.

"So you mean, like a gun for hire?"

"In your Wild West parlance," she said, "yes."

"I'm not interested in dueling with a substitute," Clint said.

"Then perhaps you should have another meeting with him," Marguerite said, "to get this all straightened out."

"In which case, I'll probably need some backup, so I'm back where I started," he said, "meeting Boyd at my hotel."

"Well," Angelique said, standing, "I'd better go and see Francois."

"He's waiting at his office," Clint said, also standing. "You know, I really thought shooting Styles in the shoulder would settle things on that end."

"Well," Angelique said, "I guess now you know what to do next time."

"What's that?" he asked.

She and Marguerite smiled at each other and the mother said, "Shoot him between the eyes."

Chapter Forty-Three

When Clint entered his hotel, he was satisfied to see Boyd's considerable bulk dominating it.

"Glad you're here," he said.

"I was gonna contact you and the captain, anyway," Boyd said. "I have your crew."

"And she might have a ship," Clint said, "but first there's another matter."

"What would that be?" Boyd asked.

"Is there someplace quiet around here to get a drink?" Clint asked.

Boyd grinned.

"Follow me."

The big man led Clint down the street to a small saloon—it resembled the one on Canal Street, only it was clean.

"Hey, Boyd!" the bartender greeted as he walked in.

"Are you known in all the saloons in New Orleans?" Clint asked.

"Just the ones in the French Quarter with, uh, questionable reputations. Roland, two beers, in the corner."

"Comin' up."

The place was full, but Clint could see that the corner table Boyd was talking about was sitting there, empty and waiting. The big man greeted several of the customers as they walked among them.

They sat and Roland came over with the two beers.

"First," Clint said, "tell me about the crew."

"We've got everybody we need, including the cabin boy," Boyd said. "They're all willing to take orders from Captain Angelique."

"Okay," Clint said. "Now I've got another problem."

"What's that?"

"His name is Styles."

"What happened between you and Styles?"

"I shot him."

"Good!" Boyd said. "It's about time somebody killed that old thief."

"I didn't kill him. I shot him in the shoulder."

"Oh," Boyd said, "that's bad."

"Why?"

"Because he won't stand for that."

"Will he go to the law?"

"Oh no," Boyd said, "he'll send somebody to handle it for him."

"Hired help?"

"Definitely," Boyd said, "but if you shot him, then he's gonna wanna be there to watch."

"Well," Clint said, "it seems like I may need a little backup."

"You've got it."

"Already?"

"The crew," Boyd said. "They're prepared to be pirates, so this won't be a problem. They can handle both."

"So when do we all get together?" Clint asked.

"We're gonna want to see the ship," Boyd said. "When do we do that?"

"Angelique is making arrangements right now," Clint said.

"Okay, then," Boyd said. "Let's meet at the same place tonight, on Canal Street."

"All of us?" Clint asked. "The crew?"

"No," Boyd said, "you, me and the Cap'n. We'll make arrangements for all of us to meet on the ship. How's that sound?"

"Sounds fine."

"As for you and your backup, I can have a couple of friends of mine at your hotel tonight, just to keep an eye out for you."

"That'll work, too," Clint said.

"Then I'll see you and Angelique tonight," Boyd said, and they clinked glasses.

Chapter Forty-Four

When Clint got to Canal Street, he saw that he was the first. He secured a table in the back of the crowded saloon. The other customers didn't pay much attention to him. He assumed since he had been there with Boyd, he was accepted.

But they did pay attention when Angelique walked in. She stopped just inside, then saw Clint when he stood up. As she crossed the room, she did so with a little extra hip-sway, as she knew she was being observed by everyone.

"Drink?" Clint asked.

"I'll just have a beer," she said.

Clint went to the bar and came back with two beers.

"How did it go?" he asked. "With Bouchet, I mean?"

"Perfectly," she said. "He found me a three-master."

"When can you pick it up?"

"Tomorrow," she said. "In a small cove near Algiers."

"Algiers?"

"Yes," she said. "It's just across the river. We'll need to take the ferry across. How did it go with Boyd?"

"He's got the whole crew, and they'll back me up if the need arises," Clint said.

"Will the crew be here tonight?"

"No," he said, "Boyd's coming, but you'll see your crew tomorrow. You'll just have to tell Boyd where they should meet you."

"Me?"

"Well, us," Clint said. "I've come this far, I want to see the boat."

"Ship."

"Right."

"And will you be coming along when we put out to sea?" she asked.

"No, I don't think so. I like to keep my feet on dry land."

"I thought you would be coming to Barataria Bay with me."

"Can't do it," he said. "But I'll tell you where to drop me a line and let me know what you found."

"I was hoping you would continue to watch out for me," Angelique said.

"Captain," he said, "you're going to have a whole crew for that."

At that moment Boyd entered, stopped at the bar for a beer, and then joined them.

"Nobody's across the street," he told Clint. "I sent my boys home."

"Let's hope it stays that way."

"Captain," Boyd said to Angelique, "I hear we have a ship."

"Let me tell you about it," she said.

***

Marguerite Laffite was admitted to the Bouchet home by the house man, Zachary.

"Mademoiselle," he said, "this way."

Zachary showed her to the sitting room, where Francois and Eloise were enjoying a drink.

"Marguerite, darling," Ellie said. "Welcome. Brandy?"

"Why not?"

Ellie poured and handed Marguerite the glass.

"A toast," Francois Bouchet said, raising his glass, "to Captain Angelique Laffite."

They all drank.

"So it went well?" she asked.

"Your daughter has her ship," Bouchet said, "and no idea that you had anything to do with it."

"Thank you, Frankie," Marguerite said.

"It was very kind of you to arrange for your daughter to become a pirate," Ellie said.

Marguerite smiled.

"Any mother would have done the same," she said.

Chapter Forty-Five

In the morning Clint and Angelique took a carriage from Clint's hotel—where she had spent the night—to the Algiers ferry at the base of Canal Street. This ferry had been running since eighteen-twenty-seven.

When they got to the other end, a carriage was waiting, having been previously arranged by Francois Bouchet. When they arrived at the cove, there was a flurry of activity, both on and around a three-masted ship.

"So that's a barque," Clint said.

"That's it," Angelique said.

She was wearing tight trousers, almost hip high boots, a blue silk shirt with puffed sleeves. She was dressed for the part, her long black hair held back by a blue scarf.

"Let's go and meet your crew," Clint said.

They headed down the dock toward the ship, able to easily pick out Boyd among all the others. The big man stood out.

"Good-mornin', Captain," Boyd greeted.

"Mr. Boyd," she said. "I assume our crew is all here?"

"Here and ready for our maiden voyage, Cap'n," Boyd said.

"It'll just be a test run today, Mr. Boyd," she told him.

"That's fine, Cap'n," he said. "We're ready." Then his eyes drifted past Clint and Angelique. "What the—"

Clint turned and saw several wagons pulling to a stop behind the carriage he and Angelique had taken. Men began to pour out, then waited for a final man to step down. That man strode down the dock alone, one arm in a sling.

"Did you really think anything goes on in New Orleans concerning boats that I wouldn't know about?" Paul Styles asked.

The crew on the boat and the dock all stopped to watch.

"What do you want, Styles?" Clint asked.

"You didn't think I was just gonna let you get away with putting a bullet in me, did you, Adams?"

"I guess I should've done what a friend of mine told me," Clint said.

"What's that?"

"Put the bullet between your eyes."

"Maybe you should have."

"Well," Clint said, taking his gun from his belt, "I could fix that now."

"Won't do you any good," Styles said. "My men will still tear this ship apart, along with the crew."

Styles turned and looked at his men, who were suddenly brandishing knives and clubs. They were all dressed like dock workers.

"I don't think so, Mr. Styles," Boyd said.

"Who're you?"

"I'm the Quartermaster of this ship," Boyd said, "and our crew is ready for anythin'."

"Show him, Mr. Boyd," Angelique said.

"Yes, Cap'n."

Boyd waved and suddenly the crew members, both on the ship and the dock, were brandishing cutlasses. Boyd also brought one out and handed it to Angelique.

"This is yours, Cap'n," he said.

"Thank you, Mr. Boyd," she said, accepting it. She stepped up to stand next to Clint.

"Whenever you're ready, Styles," Clint said.

"You people are crazy," Styles said. "I've had a long-time interest in Barataria Bay, *Captain*, and I'm not about to let you get there first."

"It's my grandfather's legacy we're talking about, Mr. Styles," Angelique said. "Who is more entitled to it than I am?"

"You and your mother are no more related to Jean Laffite than I!" he snapped.

"All these men are getting restless, Styles," Clint said. "It's your call. Just remember . . . between the eyes, this time."

"You're bluffing," Styles said. "You wouldn't dare. Not in front of all these witnesses. I'm unarmed."

"All these armed witnesses, you mean?" Clint asked.

"Clint," Angelique said, "let us handle it. This is my business."

Clint looked at Angelique.

"Are you sure?" he asked.

"Very," she said, stepping in front of Clint. "Mr. Styles, if your men want to put their knives and clubs up against our cutlasses, tell them to come ahead. The crew of the *Jean Laffite* is ready."

"Wait," Clint said, "let me step out of the way with Mr. Styles."

"Go ahead," she said.

Clint moved closer to Styles and pointed the gun at his face.

"Let's go, Styles," Clint said. "We'll watch the action from a distance."

"You can't—"

Now Clint pointed the gun at Styles' knee.

"Move!" he said.

Styles turned and walked back up the dock towards his men, with Clint close behind.

Chapter Forty-Six

Clint walked Styles past his men, who all stood and watched, waiting for their boss's word to do something.

They got well off to one side, on the road, before they turned and looked back. All the men—Styles' at one end of the deck, and Angelique's pirate crew at the other—were just waiting for the word, from anybody.

"Your men will be cut to pieces by those cutlasses," Clint told Styles. "Is that what you want?"

"I want what's on that island in Barataria Bay," Styles said.

"What makes you think anything is there?" Clint asked.

"It's the legend," Styles said.

"Legends aren't real," Clint said.

"They can be," Styles argued.

"Well then," Clint said, "they're all waiting for you to give the word."

Before Styles could say anything else, they heard horses approaching. Clint turned and saw two buckboards loaded with soldiers coming up the road. They drew to a stop and all the men, armed with rifles, jumped down. They ran over and surrounded Styles' men.

A man wearing Lieutenant's bars on his blue jacket came over to Clint and said, "It's all right, Mr. Adams. I'm Lieutenant Rayburn. We'll take it from here."

"What's going on, Lieutenant?" Clint asked.

The soldier pointed and said, "There's somebody who can explain it to you, sir. You can put the gun away."

"What the hell—" Styles said.

"Mr. Styles," Rayburn said, "you're under arrest." He turned and shouted, "Round up these men!"

The soldiers began to disarm Styles' men.

Clint put his gun in his belt and looked across the road where the Lieutenant had pointed. He saw Nina standing there. She waved him over.

"What's going on, Nina?" he asked, as he approached her. She was wearing jeans and a man's work shirt.

"Ever since Jean Laffite helped Andrew Jackson win the Battle of New Orleans, the government has known there was something out at Barataria Bay. We just needed somebody to find it. That's why I was put in Marguerite's house."

"So you're with the government," Clint said. "Working undercover?"

The soldiers were loading the prisoners onto the buckboards.

"For a couple of years, now," she said. "But Washington was getting tired of waiting—until you came along."

"I didn't have anything to do with this," Clint said.

"I think you did," Nina said. "I think you helped push Angelique over the edge, so that she realized her pirate dream."

"And now?" Clint asked, waving his arm. "What's all this about?"

"Washington wants her to go and find her grandfather's legacy," Nina said.

"They believe she's really Laffite's granddaughter?"

"Whether she is or isn't, they think she can find it."

"Why?"

Nina smiled.

"Because I told them she's just stubborn enough to do it."

"And they took your word for that?"

"They trusted me enough to put me in here," she said. "So, yes, they did."

The Lieutenant came over to them.

"We got 'em all, Ma'am."

"Good," she said. "Then your work is done here. Take them all in."

"What are we charging them with?"

"Styles is a thief, we all know that," she said. "We'll think of something."

"And them?" He waved at the pirate crew, who were still standing with their cutlasses in their hands.

"Leave them be," she said.

"Yes, Ma'am."

He turned and walked to one of the buckboards, and both of the wagons started off, with soldiers running along each side.

"There you go," she said. "It's all over. You can tell Captain Laffite she can get on with it."

"And what will you do when she finds what she's looking for?" Clint asked. "What will the government do?"

"I guess we'll decide if it's also what we're looking for," she answered. "If not, I guess it'll be hers. It's more likely none of us will end up with a thing."

"Is that your opinion?"

"That's my opinion," she said. "I'll leave it to you to tell your girlfriend."

"She's not my girlfriend."

"Then Marguerite?" Nina asked. "Or Ellie Bouchet?"

"None of them," Clint said. "And I'll be leaving New Orleans, probably tomorrow."

"Then I guess none of them would mind if I came by your room tonight," she said. "you know, just to say goodbye."

"I don't know about them," Clint said, "but I don't think I'd mind it, at all."

"See you then," she said, and walked away. It was possible she intended to walk all the way to the ferry. He thought about following her—she interested him—but he decided he better go and talk with Angelique, let her know her crew could stand down and go back to getting ready for their maiden voyage.

He had no idea what was going to happen out at Barataria Bay, but maybe some time in the future he would hear about it.

Coming March 27, 2020

THE GUNSMITH
457
The Guns of St. Augustine

**For more information
click here:** www.SpeakingVolumes.us

On Sale Now!

THE GUNSMITH
455
Brotherly Love

For more information
visit: www.SpeakingVolumes.us

On Sale Now!

THE GUNSMITH *series*
Books 430 – 454

**For more information
visit:**

Coming Soon!

Lady Gunsmith
9
Roxy Doyle and the Lady Executioner

For more information
visit: www.SpeakingVolumes.us

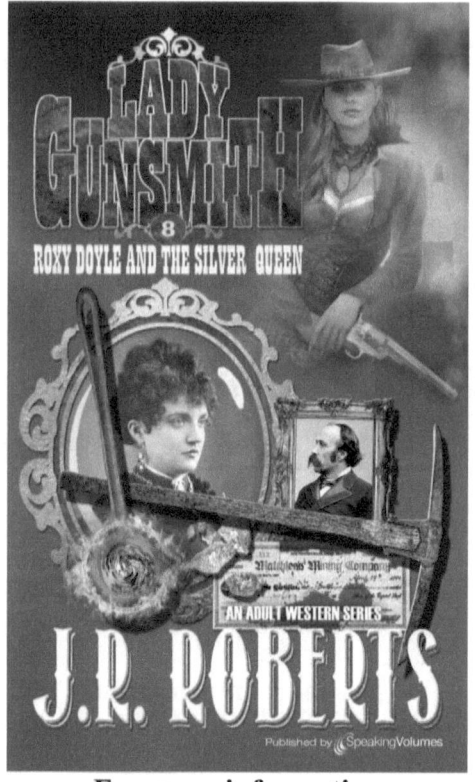